TRISTYN BARBERI

Curious Cinders

First published by TB Press 2025

Copyright © 2025 by Tristyn Barberi

All rights reserved. No part of this publication may be reproduced, stored or transmitted in any form or by any means, electronic, mechanical, photocopying, recording, scanning, or otherwise without written permission from the publisher. It is illegal to copy this book, post it to a website, or distribute it by any other means without permission.

This novel is entirely a work of fiction. The names, characters and incidents portrayed in it are the work of the author's imagination. Any resemblance to actual persons, living or dead, events or localities is entirely coincidental.

First edition

This book was professionally typeset on Reedsy. Find out more at reedsy.com

Contents

Chapter 1	1
Chapter 2	8
Chapter 3	14
Chapter 4	20
Chapter 5	27
Chapter 6	31
Chapter 7	35
Chapter 8	39
Chapter 9	43
Chapter 10	47
Chapter 11	51
Chapter 12	55
Chapter 13	59
Chapter 14	64
Chapter 15	69
Chapter 16	75
Chapter 17	78
Chapter 18	82
Chapter 19	85
Chapter 20	89
Chapter 21	96
Chapter 22	102
Chapter 23	107
Chapter 24	112

Chapter 25	116
Chapter 26	121
Chapter 27	127
Chapter 28	133
Chapter 29	140
Chapter 30	145
Chapter 31	151
Chapter 32	162
Chapter 33	169
Chapter 34	174
Chapter 35	178
Also By Tristyn Barberi	181
About the Author	182

Chapter 1

The hum of the fluorescent lights above Gideon Croft's desk was a monotonous, low-frequency drone, a sound he'd come to associate with the slow, agonizing decay of his journalistic soul. It was 9:07 AM on a Tuesday, and the Oakhaven Gazette's newsroom, a cavernous space designed for a bustling metropolis but occupied by a skeletal crew of three, was already steeped in the quiet desperation of another unremarkable day. Dust motes danced in the anemic sunlight filtering through the grimy window, illuminating the forgotten stacks of old newspapers and the faint, lingering scent of stale coffee and unfulfilled ambition.

Gideon, thirty-two years old and already feeling the encroaching weariness of a man twice his age, stared at the blinking cursor on his screen. His fingers hovered over the keyboard, but the words refused to materialize. He was supposed to be crafting a compelling narrative about the upcoming annual 'Pumpkin Patch Parade' – a story so devoid of actual news that it felt like a cruel joke from the universe. His editor, a perpetually harried woman named Brenda who seemed to subsist solely on lukewarm tea and the fading glory of a single Pulitzer nomination from the early 90s, had given him a strict word count and an even stricter deadline. "Make it pop, Gideon," she'd chirped that morning, her voice laced with an optimism that Gideon found deeply unsettling. "Think community spirit! Think autumnal charm!"

He snorted, a barely audible sound that was swallowed by the oppressive silence. Community spirit. Autumnal charm. These were the phrases that haunted his waking hours, the saccharine syrup that coated every story he wrote for the *Gazette*. He, Gideon Croft, who had once dreamt of breaking international scandals, of exposing corruption, of writing the kind of hard-hitting prose that changed minds and sparked revolutions, was now the undisputed king of local bake sale announcements and lost pet notices.

His cynicism wasn't a recent development; it was a carefully cultivated defense mechanism, honed over years of disappointment. He'd arrived in Oakhaven five years ago, fresh out of a prestigious journalism program, brimming with idealism and a portfolio full of fiery investigative pieces from his college newspaper. He'd envisioned Oakhaven as a stepping stone, a quaint, quiet town where he could cut his teeth on smaller, yet still meaningful, stories before leaping to a major metropolitan paper.

He'd been wrong. Oakhaven wasn't a stepping stone; it was a quicksand pit, slowly but surely swallowing his aspirations. Nothing happened here. Absolutely nothing. The biggest scandal in recent memory involved a misplaced garden gnome and a heated debate at the town council meeting over the optimal shade of beige for the new municipal building. Gideon had covered both with a straight face, his internal monologue a constant, screaming protest.

He glanced at his watch. 9:15 AM. Eight hours until he could escape this purgatory. He sighed, a deep, theatrical exhalation that earned him a quick, annoyed glance from Martha, the *Gazette's* octogenarian obituary writer, who was meticulously cross-referencing death dates with birth charts. Martha, a creature of habit and a connoisseur of the macabre, was the only person in the office who seemed genuinely content with her lot. Gideon often wondered if she knew something he didn't, or if her soul had simply atrophied beyond the point of feeling boredom.

He forced himself to type. "Oakhaven residents are eagerly anticipating the vibrant spectacle of the annual Pumpkin Patch Parade, a beloved tradition that promises to paint Main Street in hues of orange and gold..." He paused, his gaze drifting out the window. A lone squirrel chased another up a maple tree, its tail a blur of frantic energy. Even the squirrels in Oakhaven seemed to have more purpose than he did.

His phone buzzed. It was his mother. He let it go to voicemail. She'd call again. She always did. Her calls were a weekly reminder of the life he hadn't lived, the expectations he hadn't met. "Still chasing those big stories, Gideon?" she'd ask, her voice laced with a thinly veiled disappointment. "Or are you still writing about prize-winning zucchini?"

He ran a hand through his perpetually messy dark hair. He needed a story. A real story. Something with teeth, with stakes, with a pulse. Not another saccharine ode to seasonal gourds. He opened a new tab on his browser, habitually checking the national news feeds, scrolling through headlines of political turmoil, economic crises, and international intrigue. A pang of envy, sharp and familiar, twisted in his gut. That was where he belonged. In the thick of it, uncovering truths, holding power accountable. Not here, documenting the minutiae of small-town life.

He closed the tab with a frustrated click. It was a pointless exercise. The *Gazette* wouldn't greenlight anything beyond the local dog show. Brenda's mantra was "keep it light, keep it local, keep it inoffensive." His last attempt to pitch an investigative piece on the suspiciously low bids for the town's new bridge project had been met with a blank stare and a suggestion that he focus on the upcoming 'Annual Apple Pie Bake-Off' instead. "People want comfort, Gideon," she'd said, sipping her tea. "Not controversy."

Comfort. That was Oakhaven's defining characteristic. A town built on comfort, on predictability, on the unspoken agreement that nothing truly bad, or truly interesting, would ever happen within its neatly trimmed hedges and freshly painted picket fences. The days bled into one another, indistinguishable in their quiet monotony. The biggest excitement was the weekly delivery of fresh produce to the general store, or the occasional minor fender bender at the intersection of Main and Elm.

Gideon leaned back in his creaky office chair, the worn leather groaning in protest. He remembered the thrill of his first byline, a scathing exposé on campus housing conditions that had actually led to reforms. He'd felt a surge of power, a sense of purpose. Now, the only surge he felt was the caffeine crash after his third cup of lukewarm coffee.

He picked up a crumpled flyer from his desk. "Oakhaven Historical Society Presents: A Glimpse into Our Glorious Past!" Another assignment. He was supposed to write a preview. He imagined the article: a dry recitation of dates and names, interspersed with platitudes about community heritage. His mind already felt numb.

He stood up and stretched, his joints popping in protest. He walked over to the communal coffee maker, a relic from the

CHAPTER 1

1980s that wheezed and sputtered with every brew. As he waited for the lukewarm liquid to drip into his mug, he overheard Martha on the phone, her voice a low murmur. "Yes, dear, a lovely service. And such a beautiful casket. Polished to a shine, it was." Gideon suppressed a shiver. Even death in Oakhaven sounded... comfortable.

He returned to his desk, the aroma of burnt coffee doing little to invigorate him. He stared at the blank space beneath his opening paragraph about the Pumpkin Patch Parade. What could he possibly say that hadn't been said a hundred times before? How could he make "vibrant spectacle" sound anything other than utterly dull?

His gaze fell upon a small, framed photograph on his desk. It was a picture of him, younger, more vibrant, holding up a copy of his college newspaper with his first big story on the front page. His eyes in the photo sparkled with an almost naive hope. He looked at himself now, reflected faintly in the dark screen of his computer monitor. The sparkle was gone, replaced by a weary resignation.

He thought of his peers from journalism school, scattered across the country, some working for major news outlets, others embedded in war zones, chasing stories that mattered. He imagined them, fueled by adrenaline and purpose, while he sat here, contemplating the existential dread of a pumpkin.

A sudden, faint glint caught his eye. It was coming from the corner of the room, near the dusty filing cabinets. A small, almost imperceptible shimmer. He blinked, thinking it was just the light playing tricks, or perhaps a stray piece of tinfoil. But then it moved, a tiny flash, like a distant star winking out.

He frowned, his journalistic instincts, long dormant, stirring faintly. It was too small to be anything significant, probably just a trick of the light, but it was *something*. Something out of the ordinary in a place where ordinary was the highest law.

He pushed his chair back, the creak echoing in the quiet office. He walked slowly towards the filing cabinets, his eyes fixed on the spot where he'd seen the glimmer. As he got closer, he saw it again, a fleeting sparkle, then another, almost like tiny, errant fireflies. He bent down, peering into the shadows behind the last cabinet.

Nothing. Just dust bunnies and forgotten paperclips.

He straightened up, shaking his head. He was losing it. The Oakhaven Blues were getting to him, making him see things. He was so desperate for a story, for *anything* interesting, that his mind was conjuring phantom glimmers.

He turned to go back to his desk, to the pumpkin parade, to the suffocating normalcy of his life. But then, from the very edge of his peripheral vision, he saw it again. A distinct, almost playful flash, this time from *under* the filing cabinet. It was undeniably there. And it was moving.

A flicker of something akin to curiosity, a sensation he hadn't felt in years, pricked at him. It wasn't a story, not yet. But it was a distraction, a brief reprieve from the soul-crushing boredom. He knelt down, pulling out his phone and activating its flashlight. He aimed the beam under the cabinet.

The light illuminated a small, dark crevice. And then, he saw it. Not a piece of tinfoil. Not a trick of the light.

A tiny, iridescent scale, no bigger than his thumbnail, lay nestled amongst the dust. As he watched, a faint wisp of smoke, almost invisible, curled up from the shadows, dissipating into the stale office air. And then, a sound. A faint, almost musical *clink*, as if something impossibly small had just dropped a coin.

Gideon Croft, the cynical journalist, the man who believed

CHAPTER 1

nothing could surprise him anymore, felt a jolt of pure, unadulterated shock. His heart, which had been beating to the slow, predictable rhythm of Oakhaven, suddenly hammered against his ribs. This was not a pumpkin. This was not a bake sale. This was something else entirely. And for the first time in a very long time, Gideon Croft felt a flicker of something he hadn't realized he'd missed: excitement.

Chapter 2

The faint, almost musical *clink* under the filing cabinet echoed in Gideon Croft's ears long after he'd straightened up, his knees protesting the sudden movement. Excitement, a raw, almost forgotten sensation, fizzed through his veins. He glanced around the newsroom. Martha was still engrossed in her morbid cross-referencing, humming a tuneless dirge. Brenda's office door was ajar, but she was on the phone, her voice a low, exasperated drone. No one had noticed his strange detour.

He returned to his desk, but the Pumpkin Patch Parade article now seemed utterly absurd. How could he possibly focus on autumnal charm when he'd just seen... what had he seen? A tiny, iridescent scale. A wisp of smoke. A sound like a miniature coin dropping. His mind raced, trying to find a rational explanation. A lizard? A particularly sparkly beetle? The smoke was the sticking point. No beetle, no lizard, produced smoke. And the scale... it had felt too smooth, too perfect, too *unnatural*.

He pulled out his phone again, not to write, but to search. "Tiny iridescent scale," he typed, then added, "smoke." The results were a predictable mix of fantasy forums, New Age crystal shops, and articles about rare minerals. Nothing about living creatures. He tried "miniature smoke-producing animal." More fantasy, more crystals. His rational mind screamed

CHAPTER 2

at him, told him he was being ridiculous. It was probably just dust, or a trick of the light, or a piece of plastic from a forgotten toy. But the *clink*...

He spent the rest of the morning in a haze, mechanically typing out paragraphs about pumpkin carving contests and hayrides, his gaze constantly drifting towards the filing cabinets. Every shadow seemed to hold a secret, every creak of the old building sounded like a tiny, unseen movement. He even imagined he caught a faint, metallic scent, like ozone after a lightning strike, but dismissed it as his imagination running wild.

Just as the clock crawled towards noon, Brenda's voice cut through the quiet. "Gideon! My office. Now."

He braced himself. Had she noticed his distraction? Was he about to be reprimanded for his lack of enthusiasm for gourds? He pushed himself up, the excitement from earlier replaced by a familiar dread.

Brenda sat behind her cluttered desk, a half-eaten granola bar beside her lukewarm tea. Her usually harried expression was replaced by one of mild bewilderment. "Gideon, I have a new assignment for you."

He nodded, resigned. "The Annual Pet Show? The Town Council's new recycling initiative?"

She waved a dismissive hand. "No, no. Something... odder. Mrs. Gable just called. Again."

Mrs. Gable. The town's resident eccentric, known for her prize-winning petunias and her even more prized collection of antique thimbles. Gideon felt a flicker of something. Mrs. Gable was usually a source of amusing, if ultimately trivial, local color.

"What's happened?" he asked, trying to sound professional.

"Her thimbles," Brenda said, rubbing her temples. "All of

them. Gone. Vanished. She swears they were on display in her curio cabinet last night, and this morning, poof. Not a single one."

Gideon raised an eyebrow. "All of them? That's... a lot of thimbles."

"Indeed. Over sixty, she claims. Silver, gold, mother-of-pearl, some with tiny gemstones. Apparently, they're quite valuable. Or at least, valuable to her." Brenda sighed. "Chief Miller just left. He's already dismissed it as a prank. Kids, probably. Or she misplaced them. You know Mrs. Gable."

Gideon did know Mrs. Gable. She was meticulous, almost obsessively so, about her thimbles. Misplacing one would be an anomaly; misplacing sixty was unthinkable. "And you want me to...?"

"A filler piece," Brenda said, gesturing vaguely. "Something light. 'Local Oddities: The Case of the Missing Thimbles.' Make it charming. A little mystery. We can run it next to the Pumpkin Parade piece. People love a good, harmless enigma."

Harmless. Gideon felt a chill. He thought of the iridescent scale, the wisp of smoke, the tiny *clink*. Was it possible? Could this be... connected? It was a wild, illogical leap, but the thought had taken root.

"Sure, Brenda," he said, trying to keep his voice even. "I'll get right on it."

He left her office, a strange mix of dread and exhilaration swirling within him. This was it. This was his chance to investigate something, anything, that wasn't a vegetable or a municipal ordinance. Even if it was just a "local oddity."

His first stop was Mrs. Gable's Victorian-era house, a gingerbread-trimmed confection perched on a hill overlooking Oakhaven. The air inside was thick with the scent of lavender

CHAPTER 2

and old lace. Mrs. Gable, a spry woman with a bun of white hair and eyes that missed nothing, met him at the door, wringing her hands.

"Oh, Mr. Croft, thank goodness you're here! The police, bless their hearts, they just don't understand. My thimbles! My precious thimbles!"

She led him into her parlor, a room crammed with antiques and curios. The curio cabinet, a dark wood piece with glass doors, stood empty. Gideon examined it. No forced entry, no broken glass. It was as if the thimbles had simply dematerialized.

"Tell me exactly what happened, Mrs. Gable," Gideon said, pulling out his notepad. He tried to sound sympathetic, but his mind was already cataloging details, looking for inconsistencies, for anything out of the ordinary.

"Well," she began, her voice trembling slightly, "I always polish them every evening before bed. A little ritual, you see. And last night, they were all there, sparkling. Every single one. I locked the cabinet, just like always. And this morning, when I went to admire them with my tea... gone! Poof!"

"Did you hear anything unusual last night?" Gideon pressed. "Any sounds? A disturbance?"

She paused, her brow furrowed in thought. "Hmm. Now that you mention it... I did hear a faint tinkling sound. Like tiny bells. I thought it was just the wind chimes outside, but it was... different. And then, just for a moment, I smelled something. Like... like a tiny bonfire. But it was gone so quickly, I thought I imagined it."

Gideon's hand paused over his notepad. Tiny bells. Tiny bonfire. His heart throbbed. This was too specific. Too close to what he'd experienced in the office. He forced himself to remain calm, to not let his excitement show.

"And the windows? Doors?" he asked, gesturing around the room.

"All locked up tight," she confirmed. "I'm very careful, Mr. Croft. Very careful indeed. No one could have gotten in."

He spent another hour at Mrs. Gable's, meticulously documenting every detail, taking photographs of the empty cabinet. He even checked the fireplace, the chimney, any small opening that a human thief might have overlooked. Nothing. It was a clean, impossible disappearance.

His next stop was the Oakhaven Police Department, a small, brick building next to the town hall. Chief Miller, a portly man with a perpetually tired expression and a fondness for donuts, was behind his desk, filling out paperwork.

"Ah, Gideon," he said, waving him in. "Here about the Gable thimbles, I presume? Brenda called. Said you were doing a human interest piece."

"That's right, Chief," Gideon replied, pulling up a chair. "Just trying to get the official police perspective."

Chief Miller chuckled, shaking his head. "Official perspective is, it's a prank. Or Mrs. Gable's getting a bit forgetful. No signs of forced entry. No witnesses. No motive. Who steals thimbles, Gideon? Kids, probably. Or maybe a disgruntled neighbor. We'll keep an eye out, of course, but honestly, it's a waste of resources."

"Did Mrs. Gable mention anything about strange sounds?" Gideon asked casually, trying to gauge Miller's reaction. "Or a peculiar smell?"

Miller waved a dismissive hand. "Old Mrs. Gable's imagination, bless her heart. She said something about tiny bells and a whiff of smoke. Probably just the wind and her furnace kicking on. Nothing concrete, Gideon. Nothing to go on."

Gideon pressed no further. He knew Miller wouldn't believe him if he suggested anything else. The Chief was a man of logic, of the tangible. A tiny dragon with a penchant for shiny objects would be far beyond his capacity for belief.

He left the police station, the Oakhaven sun feeling strangely warm on his face. The town still looked the same, sleepy and unremarkable. But to Gideon, it felt different. The air hummed with a new, secret energy. The mundane façade had cracked, just a sliver, and through it, he'd glimpsed something extraordinary.

He drove back to the *Gazette* office, his mind buzzing. He had a story. Not the Pumpkin Patch Parade. Not the Apple Pie Bake-Off. He had a real story. A mystery. A bizarre, impossible crime. And he had a prime suspect, even if that suspect was currently nothing more than an iridescent scale and a wisp of smoke under a filing cabinet.

He pulled into his parking spot, the old engine sputtering to a halt. He looked up at the *Gazette* building, its faded sign proclaiming "Oakhaven's Trusted Source for Local News." He smiled, a genuine, unforced smile that hadn't touched his lips in years.

He had a feeling Oakhaven was about to get a lot less comfortable. And he, Gideon Croft, was finally going to write about something that mattered. Even if no one else believed him yet.

Chapter 3

The *Gazette* office felt different to Gideon Croft the next morning. The fluorescent hum was still there, the dust motes still danced, and Martha still muttered about astrological charts and funeral arrangements, but Gideon felt a prickle of anticipation, a nervous energy that had been absent for years. He'd submitted his "Local Oddities" piece on Mrs. Gable's thimbles, a carefully worded article that hinted at mystery without explicitly suggesting tiny, fire-breathing culprits. Brenda had given it a cursory glance and a nod of approval, completely missing the subtle undertones Gideon had woven in.

He was sipping his truly terrible coffee, trying to ignore the blandness of his Pumpkin Patch Parade draft, when the first call came in. It was from the Oakhaven Diner, a greasy spoon institution that served the town's best (and only) breakfast.

"Gideon, you gotta get down here!" croaked Sal, the diner's owner, his voice thick with exasperation. "My lucky spatula! The one with the shiny, polished handle! It's gone! And... and there's a burn mark on the counter. Small, but definitely a burn!"

Gideon's hand tightened around his coffee mug. A burn mark. He felt a surge of adrenaline. "I'm on my way, Sal."

CHAPTER 3

He grabbed his notepad and camera, a renewed sense of purpose propelling him out of the office. He didn't bother telling Brenda where he was going. She'd just tell him to stick to pumpkins.

The Oakhaven Diner smelled of stale grease and burnt toast. Sal, a man whose apron seemed to be a permanent extension of his body, was gesturing wildly at a small, circular scorch mark on the stainless steel counter. It was no bigger than a quarter, perfectly round, and looked as if a miniature, intensely hot coin had been pressed against the surface.

"See, Gideon? Right here! And the spatula was sitting right next to it! My lucky spatula! Used it for twenty years!" Sal wrung his hands, leaving greasy smudges on his apron. "Chief Miller just left. Said it was probably a cigarette burn and I misplaced the spatula. Misplaced it! I never misplace anything!"

Gideon knelt, examining the scorch mark. It was identical in character to the faint scent of "tiny bonfire" Mrs. Gable had described. He took several photos, then carefully measured the diameter of the mark. He asked Sal about any unusual sounds or smells, but Sal, still fixated on his missing spatula, could only recall the usual diner cacophony.

As he was leaving the diner, his phone rang again. This time, it was Mr. Henderson, the town's notoriously grumpy retired watchmaker.

"Croft! You that reporter fella, ain't ya?" Henderson's voice was a gravelly rumble. "My great-grandpappy's pocket watch! Gone! And there's a funny mark on my workbench!"

Gideon felt a thrill. "I'm on my way, Mr. Henderson."

Henderson's workshop was a cramped, dusty space filled with the faint ticking of countless clocks and the smell of oil and old metal. He pointed a trembling finger at his workbench. Another scorch mark, this one slightly oval, marred the polished wood. Beside it, an empty velvet cushion where the heirloom pocket watch, famously crafted from polished silver and intricate gears, had rested.

"See that, Croft? A burn! And the watch was right there! Never moved it! And that mark... it's not from my soldering iron, I tell ya! It's too... clean." Henderson squinted. "And last night, I swear I heard a faint ringing. Like little bells, but... not quite. And a whiff of something... like a tiny firecracker going off. Thought I was just imagining things, old age, you know."

Gideon's pulse quickened. Tiny bells. Tiny firecracker. This was more than coincidence. This was a pattern. A distinct, peculiar pattern. He took more photos, measurements, and listened intently to Henderson's agitated recounting. He noted the precision of the scorch marks, almost as if they were deliberately placed, or perhaps, the result of a very precise, very small, burst of heat.

He spent the rest of the day chasing down other minor incidents that had previously seemed isolated. Mrs. Higgins, whose prize-winning rose bush had a small, inexplicable singe mark on one leaf, also reported a missing silver gardening trowel. The town librarian, Ms. Finch, found a small, circular scorch on the corner of a rare, leather-bound book, and swore she'd heard a faint "whisper of crackling" the night before, though nothing had been stolen from the library itself.

Each incident, on its own, was easily dismissed. A clumsy smoker, a misplaced item, a faulty electrical wire. But when strung together, they formed a bizarre tapestry of petty crimes and inexplicable scorch marks. And the common thread? Shiny objects. And the consistent, almost identical descriptions of faint tinkling sounds and the smell of tiny bonfires or firecrackers.

Gideon returned to the *Gazette* office late in the afternoon, his head swimming with details. He ignored Brenda's questioning glance. He sat at his desk, not to write about pumpkins, but to meticulously map out the incidents. He drew a crude map of Oakhaven, marking Mrs. Gable's house, Sal's Diner, Mr. Henderson's workshop, Mrs. Higgins's garden, the library. The locations seemed random, scattered across town. But the *nature* of the incidents was undeniably linked.

He pulled up his search history from the previous day. "Tiny iridescent scale," "smoke," "miniature smoke-producing animal." He added new keywords: "small scorch marks," "unexplained disappearances of shiny objects." The results were still dominated by fantasy and fringe science. No police blotter in the world would take him seriously.

He felt a strange mix of frustration and exhilaration. Frustration because he had no concrete proof, no smoking gun (literally, in this case), and no one would believe him. Exhilaration because this was real. This was a genuine mystery, unfolding right under the nose of Oakhaven's oblivious residents and its donut-loving police chief.

He thought back to the filing cabinet, to the tiny scale, the wisp of smoke, the *clink*. He remembered the feeling of that fleeting excitement. Now, that excitement was a full-blown obsession. He was no longer just a cynical journalist stuck in a rut; he was a detective, piecing together the fragments of an impossible puzzle.

He opened a new document on his computer, bypassing the Pumpkin Patch Parade entirely. He titled it: "Oakhaven Anomaly Log."

- Incident 1: Mrs. Gable's Missing Thimbles (60+ antique silver, gold, mother-of-pearl thimbles). Witnessed faint tinkling sound, smell of "tiny bonfire." No forced entry.
- Incident 2: Sal's Missing Spatula (shiny handle). Small, circular scorch mark on counter.
- Incident 3: Mr. Henderson's Missing Pocket Watch (heirloom, polished silver). Small, oval scorch mark on workbench. Witnessed faint ringing, smell of "tiny firecracker."
- Incident 4: Mrs. Higgins's Missing Trowel (silver). Small singe mark on rose bush leaf.
- Incident 5: Ms. Finch's Scorched Book (rare, leather-bound). Small, circular scorch on corner. Witnessed "whisper of crackling." No theft reported.

He stared at the list. The pattern was undeniable. Shiny objects disappearing. Small, precise scorch marks. And the consistent auditory and olfactory anomalies. It was too specific to be random, too bizarre to be human.

His rational mind, the one that had been so dominant for so long, was slowly being chipped away by the sheer impossibility of it all. He was starting to consider the unthinkable. A creature. A small, elusive creature with a fiery breath and an inexplicable attraction to anything that glittered.

He leaned back, a new kind of smile playing on his lips. This wasn't just a local oddity. This was something extraordinary. And he, Gideon Croft, was going to be the one to uncover it. The thought of Chief Miller's face, of Brenda's bewildered expression, when he finally presented his findings, brought a genuine, almost giddy, laugh to his lips.

The Oakhaven Blues were fading. Replaced by the curious cinders of a mystery. And Gideon Croft, for the first time in

CHAPTER 3

years, felt truly alive.

Chapter 4

The Oakhaven Anomaly Log became Gideon Croft's new bible. He kept it open on his computer screen, even while pretending to work on the interminable Pumpkin Patch Parade piece. Every new report, every whispered rumor of a missing trinket or an odd scorch mark, was meticulously added to the list. He'd started carrying a small, high-resolution camera with him everywhere, along with a measuring tape and a set of sterile evidence bags, much to the amusement of Brenda, who assumed he was just "getting into the spirit of local reporting." He even bought a small, powerful magnifying glass, feeling like a character in a pulp detective novel.

The pattern solidified with each passing day. It was always something shiny, always something small enough to be easily carried, and almost always accompanied by those distinctive, precise scorch marks. The "tiny bells" and "tiny bonfire" scents were becoming more frequently reported, though still dismissed by Chief Miller as collective hysteria or overactive imaginations. Gideon, however, was past dismissal. He was entering the realm of the unbelievable, and he felt a strange, exhilarating sense of purpose.

His apartment, once a sparsely furnished bachelor pad, was slowly transforming into a makeshift command center. Maps of

Oakhaven were tacked to the walls, crisscrossed with red string connecting incident locations. He'd even started sketching possible trajectories, trying to predict where the next "theft" might occur. His colleagues at the *Gazette* noticed his newfound energy, attributing it to a late-blooming passion for community journalism. Gideon just nodded, a small, knowing smile playing on his lips. Let them think what they wanted. He had a dragon to find.

The breakthrough came on a particularly muggy Thursday afternoon. Gideon was at his desk, staring blankly at the words "The aroma of cinnamon and pumpkin spice will fill the air..." when his phone buzzed. It was Ms. Albright, the perpetually flustered curator of the Oakhaven Historical Society.

"Mr. Croft! Oh, Mr. Croft, it's simply dreadful! The fountain! The old town fountain!" Her voice was a high-pitched squeak of distress.

Gideon grabbed his notepad. "What about the fountain, Ms. Albright?"

"The coins! All the coins! The ones people toss in for good luck! They're gone! Every single one! And... and there's a mark! A terrible, burnt mark right on the edge of the basin!"

Gideon didn't wait for her to finish. The town fountain. Neglected, yes, but a central landmark. And the coins. Shiny. This was it. This felt like the epicenter.

He practically sprinted out of the office, leaving Brenda shouting after him about a deadline. He jumped into his beat-up sedan, the engine sputtering to life with a reluctant cough. He drove faster than strictly legal through Oakhaven's quiet streets, his heart hammering against his ribs.

The fountain stood in the small, overgrown town square, its stone basin cracked and stained, its cherubic statue perpetually weeping a thin stream of murky water. A small crowd had already gathered, mostly curious onlookers and a few concerned citizens, including Ms. Albright, who was wringing her hands by the edge of the basin. Chief Miller's patrol car was parked haphazardly nearby, and the Chief himself was already there, looking exasperated.

"Honestly, Ms. Albright," Miller was saying, his voice a weary drone, "it's probably just kids. A few teenagers with a net. Happens all the time."

"But the mark, Chief! The burn mark!" Ms. Albright wailed, pointing a trembling finger.

Gideon pushed through the small crowd, his eyes immediately scanning the fountain. And there it was. On the lip of the stone basin, just above the water line, was a scorch mark. This one was larger than the others he'd seen, perhaps the size of a silver dollar, and distinctly claw-shaped, as if something with three tiny, sharp talons had briefly landed there, leaving a searing imprint. A faint, acrid scent, like burnt sugar mixed with ozone, hung in the humid air.

He knelt, ignoring the murmurs of the crowd. He took photos, measured the mark. It was undeniably fresh. And unlike the others, this one felt... deliberate. Not an accidental sneeze, but a momentary perch.

"Chief," Gideon said, his voice low, "have you checked the surrounding area? Any other marks?"

Miller sighed. "Gideon, it's kids. They probably used a lighter. I've got real crimes to worry about."

"But the pattern, Chief," Gideon pressed, standing up. "The thimbles, the spatula, the watch. All shiny. All gone. All with these marks. And the sounds, the smells..."

Miller just shook his head, already turning away to address

Ms. Albright. "We'll file a report, ma'am. But I wouldn't get your hopes up."

Gideon ignored them. He circled the fountain slowly, his gaze sweeping the ground, the nearby bushes, the gnarled branches of the ancient oak tree that shaded the square. He was looking for anything. Any clue. Any sign.

And then he saw it.

A flash. Not a reflection off a discarded candy wrapper, but a distinct, emerald green shimmer from within the dense foliage of the oak tree. It was high up, nestled in a cluster of leaves, almost perfectly camouflaged.

His breath hitched. He moved slowly, cautiously, trying not to draw attention. He raised his camera, zooming in. The leaves shifted, and for a fleeting moment, he saw it clearly.

It was tiny. No bigger than a common housecat, perhaps even smaller. Its scales were a dazzling, iridescent emerald green, catching the sunlight like scattered jewels. A pair of delicate, leathery wings, veined with gold, were folded neatly against its back. Its head was surprisingly elegant, with sharp, intelligent eyes that seemed to glow with an inner fire, and two small, spiraled horns. And from its nostrils, a faint, almost playful wisp of smoke curled upwards, dissipating into the summer air.

It was a dragon. A real, honest-to-goodness, miniature dragon.

Gideon felt a profound, almost spiritual shock. Every cynical bone in his body screamed in protest, but his eyes were seeing the undeniable truth. The missing thimbles, the scorched benches, the vanishing watches – it all clicked into place with a terrifying, exhilarating clarity.

The dragon, seemingly unaware it had been spotted, shifted, its head cocked slightly, its gaze fixed on something in the distance. And then, with a sudden, graceful unfurling of its wings, it launched itself from the branch.

"Wait!" Gideon whispered, a desperate plea.

The dragon darted through the air, a blur of emerald and gold, heading towards the narrow alleyway behind the old general store. Gideon didn't hesitate. He broke into a run, pushing past startled onlookers, ignoring Chief Miller's confused shout.

He burst into the alley, the air thick with the smell of damp concrete and forgotten garbage. The dragon was there, perched on a discarded tin can, its head tilted, its bright eyes fixed on something. Gideon stopped, trying to control his ragged breathing. He didn't want to scare it. He didn't want to lose it.

The dragon, sensing his presence, turned its head slowly. Its eyes, those intelligent, fiery eyes, met his. For a long moment, they simply stared at each other, man and mythical beast, separated by a chasm of disbelief and wonder.

Gideon slowly, carefully, extended a hand. Empty. Non-threatening. "Hey there," he murmured, his voice a little shaky. "You're... you're real."

The dragon blinked, a slow, deliberate movement. A tiny puff of smoke escaped its nostrils. It didn't fly away. It seemed to be studying him, its small head tilting from side to side.

"So, you're the one," Gideon continued, a strange, almost paternal warmth spreading through him. "The one taking all the shiny things. You're quite the little thief, aren't you?" He chuckled, a soft, disbelieving sound.

The dragon let out a faint, almost musical chirrup, a sound like tiny, polished bells. It took a single, cautious step towards him on the tin can.

Gideon felt an overwhelming sense of connection, a sudden, fierce protectiveness. This creature, this impossible, beautiful creature, was the source of all the strange events, yes, but it wasn't malicious. It was just... collecting. And it was vulnerable. If the town, if Chief Miller, if anyone else found out, it would be hunted, captured, dissected. He couldn't let that happen.

"You need a name," Gideon said, his voice barely above a whisper. "Something that fits. Something... fiery." He thought for a moment, then a word came to him, ancient and resonant. "Ingis. How about Ingis?"

The dragon, Ingis, chirruped again, a slightly louder, more joyful sound. It unfurled its wings, just a little, shimmering in the dim light of the alley. It seemed to like the name.

Gideon felt a profound shift within him. The cynical journalist, the man who had dismissed wonder, was gone. In his place was someone new, someone who had just looked into the eyes of a creature from myth and felt an undeniable pull. His journalistic instincts, the ones that screamed "scoop of the century," were suddenly silenced by a far stronger imperative: protection.

"Okay, Ingis," Gideon said, his voice firm now, resolute. "My little secret. My little fire-breather. We're going to have to figure this out. But I promise you, no one is going to hurt you."

Ingis hopped off the tin can, a tiny, graceful leap, and landed softly on the ground a few feet from Gideon's outstretched hand. It looked up at him, its intelligent eyes seeming to understand. Then, with a final, almost imperceptible puff of smoke, it turned and darted into a narrow gap between two dumpsters, disappearing from sight.

Gideon stood there for a long moment, the scent of ozone and burnt sugar still lingering in the air. His hand was still outstretched, trembling slightly. He looked back at the main street, at the oblivious crowd around the fountain, at Chief

Miller still trying to explain away the missing coins. They had no idea. No idea what was truly happening in their quiet, unremarkable town.

He, Gideon Croft, was no longer just a reporter. He was a guardian. And his life, once a monotonous drone, had just become infinitely more complicated. And infinitely more exciting. The Oakhaven Blues were not just fading; they had been incinerated by a tiny, mischievous dragon named Ingis.

Chapter 5

The alley reeked of stale beer and forgotten dreams, but to Gideon Croft, it now smelled of ozone and the impossible. He stood there, hand still outstretched, long after Ingis had vanished between the dumpsters. His mind, usually a fortress of cynicism and logical deduction, was reeling. A dragon. A miniature, emerald-scaled, smoke-puffing dragon. In Oakhaven. It was a headline so monumental, so utterly world-shattering, that his journalistic instincts should have been screaming for him to break the story.

Instead, a different, quieter voice had taken hold: *Protect it.*

He walked back to his car in a daze, the mundane sounds of Oakhaven – a distant lawnmower, Chief Miller's continued exasperated murmurs by the fountain – feeling utterly surreal. He started the engine, but instead of heading back to the *Gazette*, he drove straight to his apartment. He needed to be alone. He needed to process this.

The first thing he did was hit the internet, a frantic, desperate search. "Tiny dragons," he typed, then "miniature fire-breathing creatures," "small iridescent reptiles," "mythological beasts scientific explanation." He scoured academic journals, cryptozoology forums, even obscure folklore archives. Nothing. Absolutely nothing remotely credible or scientific.

There were plenty of fantastical tales, of course, but no verifiable accounts, no biological classifications, no mention of anything resembling Ingis. It was as if the creature he'd just seen simply did not exist.

His frustration mounted. How could something so real, so undeniably *there*, be so utterly absent from human knowledge? It was a paradox that both thrilled and terrified him. It meant Ingis was unique, perhaps the last of its kind. And that only amplified his burgeoning sense of responsibility.

He spent the next few days in a state of heightened awareness, his senses tuned to the subtle anomalies of Oakhaven. He still went to the office, still pretended to work on the Pumpkin Patch Parade, but his mind was elsewhere. He bought a pair of compact binoculars, ostensibly for "bird watching" (a new, sudden hobby he explained to Brenda), and a small, discreet notebook he kept hidden in his jacket pocket.

His mission was clear: observe Ingis. Learn its habits. Understand its world.

His initial attempts were clumsy. He'd stake out the alley behind the general store, hiding behind overflowing dumpsters, feeling utterly ridiculous. But slowly, patiently, he began to piece together Ingis's routine.

He discovered Ingis was most active during the early morning hours, just as the sun was rising, and again in the late afternoon, as shadows lengthened. It seemed to prefer the quiet times, avoiding the bustling midday. Its movements were incredibly swift and fluid, a blur of emerald and gold as it flitted between rooftops, darted through dense foliage, and occasionally, with surprising grace, landed on a high perch. It was almost impossible to track with the naked eye, hence the binoculars became indispensable.

CHAPTER 5

The "thefts" continued, providing Gideon with a breadcrumb trail. A polished, antique war medal from a veteran's display. A gleaming silver locket from a clothesline. A shiny, engraved pen from a writer's desk. Each time, Gideon would rush to the scene, pretending to be reporting for the *Gazette*, but secretly searching for the tell-tale scorch marks, the faint scent of ozone, the almost imperceptible *clink* that sometimes accompanied the disappearances. He noted that the scorch marks were always tiny, always precise, and seemed to be a byproduct of landing or taking off quickly, or perhaps, a burst of excitement.

He also learned about Ingis's preferred objects. It wasn't just *any* shiny thing; it seemed to possess an uncanny ability to discern items of *sentimental or historical value*, often those that had been cherished or passed down through generations. These items invariably possessed a particular gleam, a metallic luster, or a unique sparkle that drew Ingis in. It wasn't interested in dull plastic or painted surfaces; it had a connoisseur's taste for things that resonated with significance.

One afternoon, while observing from the relative safety of his car parked down the street from the town square, he witnessed something that melted away any lingering doubt about Ingis's nature. Ingis was perched on the weather vane of the old clock tower, its tiny form silhouetted against the setting sun. A gust of wind caught a stray autumn leaf, sending it tumbling past. Ingis, with a sudden, playful dart, chased the leaf, batting at it with a delicate claw, a tiny puff of smoke escaping its nostrils in what Gideon could only interpret as a burst of pure joy. It wasn't a monster. It was mischievous, yes, but undeniably playful, almost childlike in its curiosity.

Keeping Ingis a secret became a full-time, high-stakes endeavor. Gideon found himself subtly diverting Chief Miller's investigations, offering alternative, mundane explanations for the missing items. "Probably a magpie, Chief," he'd suggest, or "Kids these days, always up to something." He'd even gone so far as to "discover" a lost item (a less valuable, non-shiny substitute) in a conspicuous place to throw off suspicion. The guilt gnawed at him, the journalistic integrity he once held so dear now compromised by his protective instincts. But the image of Ingis, so small and vulnerable, outweighed everything else.

His apartment became a sanctuary, not just for him, but a potential safe haven for Ingis. He left out small, shiny trinkets – a polished bottle cap, a handful of pennies – hoping to lure Ingis closer, to establish a deeper trust. He'd often wake in the middle of the night, convinced he heard a faint tinkling sound from his living room, only to find nothing. Yet, sometimes, a single, newly acquired coin would appear on his desk, a silent, glittering offering.

The loneliness of his secret was immense. He couldn't tell anyone. Not Brenda, who would have him committed. Not Chief Miller, who would immediately launch a full-scale hunt. He was alone in this, the sole keeper of Oakhaven's most extraordinary secret.

But with that loneliness came a profound sense of purpose. The Oakhaven Anomaly Log was no longer just a collection of strange incidents; it was a testament to Ingis's existence, a secret history of a creature that defied all logic. Gideon, the cynical journalist, had found his story. And it was far bigger, and far more important, than anything he had ever imagined. He just had to keep it hidden. For now.

Chapter 6

The thrill of discovery, that initial rush of adrenaline from meeting Ingis, slowly began to morph into a gnawing, constant anxiety for Gideon. Keeping a tiny, mischievous, fire-breathing dragon a secret in a town as small and nosy as Oakhaven was proving to be a Herculean task. Every siren wail, every sudden knock at his door, sent a jolt of fear through him. He found himself constantly looking over his shoulder, his journalistic instincts now repurposed for espionage.

Ingis, blissfully unaware of the chaos it caused, continued its glittering spree. Its insatiable desire for shiny objects, particularly those imbued with sentimental value, seemed to intensify. A gleaming silver locket from the town's oldest resident, Mrs. Gable's prized antique thimbles (which Gideon had meticulously, and secretly, replaced with less valuable, but equally shiny, polished steel thimbles he'd bought online), Mr. Henderson's heirloom pocket watch – these were just the beginning. The Oakhaven Anomaly Log grew longer by the day, each entry a testament to Ingis's escalating boldness and Gideon's escalating panic.

Gideon's mornings now started with a quick scan of local news feeds and police blotters, not for stories to write, but for reports of new "thefts." If a particularly shiny object was reported missing, he'd drop everything, invent a flimsy excuse for Brenda, and race to the scene. His goal wasn't to report, but to *divert*.

His methods became increasingly elaborate. When the gold-plated bell from the Oakhaven Historical Society's display vanished, leaving a distinct, tiny scorch mark on its velvet cushion, Gideon arrived on the scene before Chief Miller. He quickly "noticed" a loose floorboard near the display case, subtly suggesting to Ms. Albright that perhaps a mouse had dragged the bell into a hidden cavity. He even left a few scattered mouse droppings (courtesy of a trip to a pet store) to bolster his theory. Ms. Albright, flustered but relieved, bought it completely.

Replacing stolen items was a delicate art. He couldn't just put back any shiny object; Ingis had a discerning eye. Gideon spent hours online, searching for trinkets that mimicked the original items' luster and form, but lacked their intrinsic value or sentimental history. He became an expert in costume jewelry, polished chrome, and cheap, glittering baubles. He'd then "discover" these replacements in odd places – under a bush, in a forgotten corner of a porch – suggesting they'd been dropped by a clumsy thief.

One afternoon, a frantic call came from the Oakhaven Bakery. The gleaming brass bell that hung above the counter, announcing every customer, was gone. Gideon rushed over, his heart pounding. He found the tell-tale scorch mark on the counter. While Chief Miller was distracted interviewing the baker, Gideon subtly nudged a small, shiny, but ultimately worthless, decorative spoon he'd brought with him under the counter. "Chief!" he called out, feigning surprise. "Look! Could this have been what they were after? Maybe they dropped the bell when they grabbed this?" Miller, ever eager for a simple explanation, nodded, seizing on the spoon as evidence of a common, petty thief.

The constant charade was exhausting. Gideon felt like a double agent, living a precarious existence between his public persona as a local journalist and his secret life as a dragon's protector. He had to maintain a façade of journalistic objectivity, even as he actively manipulated the narrative. He'd write articles about the "unusual string of petty thefts," framing them as a bizarre but ultimately harmless local phenomenon, attributing them to pranksters or even particularly clever squirrels. He'd subtly ridicule Fitzwilliam's "fire-breathing pixie" theories in print, even as he knew the old man was closer to the truth than anyone.

His apartment, once a sanctuary, was now a constant source of worry. He'd started leaving his balcony door slightly ajar, a silent invitation for Ingis. Sometimes, he'd find a newly acquired trinket – a shiny button, a forgotten coin – left on his desk, a silent offering from the tiny dragon. These moments, these small acts of trust, solidified his resolve. Ingis wasn't a menace; it was a creature of instinct, driven by an innate desire for beauty, and utterly unaware of the human concept of ownership.

He tried to communicate with Ingis, leaving out small, non-shiny items in exchange for the glittering ones. A smooth river stone for a stolen earring. A polished piece of driftwood for a silver thimble. Ingis seemed to understand, sometimes leaving the less valuable items untouched, other times picking them up with a curious sniff before dropping them and flying off with something more appealing. It was a slow, painstaking process of negotiation.

The biggest challenge was the scorch marks. They were harder to explain away. Gideon started carrying a small bottle of wood stain and a tiny, portable cleaning kit. If he arrived at a scene before the police, he'd quickly try to buff out or cover the marks, attributing any remaining discoloration to "old water damage" or "a faulty appliance." It was a risky game, and he knew it. One wrong move, one missed detail, and Ingis's secret would be out.

One evening, as he sat at his desk, staring at a blank screen, the weight of his secret pressed down on him. He was tired, perpetually on edge. But then, he heard a faint *clink* from his living room. He walked in to find a tiny, iridescent scale, no bigger than his pinky nail, lying on his coffee table, shimmering faintly in the lamplight. Beside it, a small, polished silver locket, one he hadn't seen before, probably a new acquisition.

He picked up the scale, its surface surprisingly warm. It was a gift. A sign of trust. He looked at the locket, then back at the scale. He knew he had to return the locket, find its owner, replace it with something less significant. But for a moment, just a moment, he held the tiny scale, a tangible piece of the impossible, and felt a surge of renewed determination.

He was Gideon Croft, journalist. And now, he was also Gideon Croft, dragon protector. The two roles were in constant conflict, but for now, the latter had undeniably taken precedence. He would keep Ingis's secret, no matter the cost. The game was on, and he was playing for the highest stakes of all.

Chapter 7

The *Gazette* office was a ghost town on Saturday. Brenda was at a regional journalism conference, Martha was undoubtedly communing with the recently departed, and Gideon Croft had, for the first time in months, a genuine day off. No Pumpkin Patch Parade to fret over, no "local oddities" to subtly misdirect. Just a blissful, quiet Saturday. And a dragon.

He'd spent the morning meticulously cleaning his apartment, a nervous habit that had intensified with Ingis's presence. He'd even bought a small, fire-resistant mat for the spot near his balcony door, just in case. The tiny iridescent scale Ingis had left him still sat on his coffee table, a tangible reminder of the impossible reality he now inhabited.

Around midday, a faint scratching sound came from the balcony door. Gideon's heart gave a familiar leap. He moved slowly, cautiously, pulling back the curtain. Ingis was perched on the railing, its emerald scales shimmering in the sunlight, its head cocked, its bright eyes fixed on him. A tiny puff of smoke curled from its nostrils, a greeting.

"Hey, Ingis," Gideon whispered, opening the door just enough for the dragon to slip inside. Ingis darted in, a blur of green, and landed gracefully on the back of his sofa. It chirped, a sound like miniature bells, and then, with a delicate flick of its tail, nudged a small, shiny silver thimble towards him. It was one of Mrs. Gable's originals, the one Gideon had failed to replace.

Gideon sighed, but a small smile touched his lips. "You know, Ingis, I'm trying to keep you a secret. And you keep taking things that make it very, very hard."

Ingis tilted its head, seemingly oblivious, then stretched, its tiny wings unfurling to their full, impressive span. As it did, a sudden, involuntary *hiccup* escaped its throat, followed by a surprisingly potent burst of flame, no bigger than a matchstick, that singed the edge of the sofa cushion.

Gideon yelped, jumping back. "Whoa! Easy there, little guy!"

Ingis seemed startled too, its eyes wide, its smoke-wisping nostrils flaring. It chirped apologetically, then rubbed its head against the singed cushion.

Gideon knelt, examining the mark. It was identical to the scorch marks he'd been cataloging all over Oakhaven. The precise, clean edges. The faint, burnt-sugar smell. It wasn't a deliberate act of arson; it was an *involuntary* reaction.

He watched Ingis closely for the rest of the afternoon. He offered it a shiny bottle cap. Ingis snatched it playfully, then, in its excitement, let out another small, fiery *sneeze* that narrowly missed Gideon's hand. Later, when Gideon accidentally dropped a pen, the sudden clatter made Ingis jump, and another tiny flame erupted, leaving a faint mark on the wooden floor.

The realization hit him with the force of a physical blow. The scorch marks weren't from Ingis landing or taking off. They were from its involuntary, fiery sneezes, triggered by sudden excitement, surprise, or perhaps even strong emotions. This explained their seemingly random placement, their varying sizes, and the fact that they often appeared *near* a stolen item, but not necessarily *on* it. Ingis wasn't setting fires; it was just... reacting.

This discovery was both a relief and a new source of anxiety. Relief, because it confirmed Ingis wasn't malicious. Anxiety, because it meant Ingis was a walking, miniature fire hazard, completely unaware of the damage it could cause. And if anyone witnessed one of these fiery sneezes, the secret would be out.

"Okay, Ingis," Gideon said, picking up the singed cushion. "We have a problem. A fiery, sneeze-shaped problem."

He spent the rest of his day off attempting to "fireproof" Ingis's favorite spots around his apartment. He moved all flammable objects away from the balcony door. He placed more fire-resistant mats on the sofa and near his desk. He even considered buying a small, portable fire extinguisher, but dismissed it as too suspicious.

His thoughts then turned to Oakhaven itself. Ingis had favorite perching spots, favorite napping places. The park bench, the bird feeder, the clock tower weather vane. These were all potential sneeze zones. He couldn't fireproof the entire town, but he could try to mitigate the risk.

The next morning, armed with a small, discreet spray bottle of fire retardant (marketed as "fabric protector"), Gideon embarked on a covert mission. He visited the park bench, pretending to be admiring the autumn leaves, and subtly sprayed the wood. He did the same with the bird feeder, claiming he was "testing a new cleaning solution." He even managed to get close enough to the clock tower base to spray a small section of the stone, hoping it would offer some protection.

He felt ridiculous, a secret agent against accidental dragon sneezes. But each act, no matter how absurd, was a testament to his commitment. He was learning Ingis's quirks, adapting to its unique existence. The dragon wasn't just a discovery; it was becoming a part of his life, a responsibility he had willingly, almost eagerly, taken on.

As the sun set on his day off, Gideon sat on his sofa, watching Ingis doze peacefully on a fire-resistant mat, a tiny wisp of smoke curling from its nostrils even in sleep. He still had Mrs. Gable's thimble on his desk, a reminder of the constant tightrope walk he was on. But now, he also had a deeper understanding of the creature he was protecting. Ingis was a creature of instinct, of beauty, and of accidental fiery sneezes. And Gideon Croft, the cynical journalist, was now its quiet, determined guardian, navigating a world where the mundane and the magical had unexpectedly collided.

Chapter 8

The revelation about Ingis's fiery sneezes, while initially alarming, had brought a new layer of understanding to Gideon's secret life. The dragon wasn't a destructive force; it was just... excitable. This knowledge, coupled with the growing sense of responsibility he felt, spurred Gideon to move beyond mere observation and damage control. He needed to build a bridge, however fragile, to the impossible creature sharing his town.

His apartment became the primary testing ground for this new endeavor. He designated a corner of his living room, near the balcony door, as Ingis's potential safe zone. He placed a soft, old blanket there, a small, shallow dish of water, and, after much deliberation, a small pile of shiny, but utterly worthless, objects: a handful of polished pennies, a few discarded bottle caps, and some crinkled aluminum foil. He hoped the foil, with its crinkly texture and bright sheen, would appeal to Ingis's magpie tendencies without causing any real loss to Oakhaven's residents.

The first attempts at direct communication were awkward, bordering on absurd. Gideon would sit on his sofa, speaking in soft, low tones, his voice a gentle murmur in the quiet apartment. "Hey, Ingis," he'd say, "it's just me. Gideon. No need to be shy." He'd try different sounds, gentle clicks of his tongue, soft whistles, anything to mimic the faint, bell-like chirps Ingis sometimes made. He felt foolish, talking to an empty room, but he persisted.

He learned quickly that direct eye contact, while not aggressive, seemed to make Ingis a little wary. A slow, deliberate blink from Gideon, however, seemed to be a sign of reassurance. He also noticed that sudden movements or loud noises would make Ingis tense, its tiny body stiffening, a wisp of smoke often escaping its nostrils. He began to move more slowly, to speak more softly, creating an atmosphere of calm whenever Ingis was near.

The shiny foil proved to be a surprising success. One evening, after a particularly frustrating day of covering a town council debate on sidewalk repairs, Gideon returned home to find a single, perfectly crinkled piece of foil sitting on his desk. It was a silent message, a sign that Ingis had visited, had accepted his offering. He felt a warmth spread through him, a small victory in his otherwise solitary mission.

He started leaving other non-valuable, shiny items: old keys, polished stones, even a piece of broken mirror. He observed Ingis's reactions. The dragon seemed to prefer the more reflective surfaces, the ones that shimmered and caught the light. It would often bat at them playfully with a claw, or nudge them with its snout, before carrying off its chosen prize.

Slowly, painstakingly, a fragile bond began to form. Ingis started visiting more frequently, sometimes perching on the back of Gideon's chair while he worked, its tiny weight a comforting presence. It would watch him with those intelligent, fiery eyes, occasionally letting out a soft chirrup that Gideon began to interpret as a sign of contentment.

One afternoon, Gideon was reading on his sofa when Ingis

flew in through the balcony door, a newly acquired, gleaming silver spoon clutched in its tiny talons. Instead of immediately darting away, Ingis landed on the armrest, chirped, and then, to Gideon's utter astonishment, gently nudged the spoon towards him. It wasn't a demand; it felt like a shared treasure.

Gideon carefully picked up the spoon, admiring its gleam. "It's beautiful, Ingis," he whispered. "But you know, someone's going to miss this."

Ingis tilted its head, then, with a delicate movement, nudged Gideon's hand with its snout. A tiny puff of smoke, almost like a sigh, escaped. Gideon, understanding the unspoken sentiment, placed the spoon back on the armrest. He would, of course, find a way to return it later, but for now, he simply shared the moment with Ingis.

This quiet interaction deepened Gideon's sense of responsibility exponentially. Ingis wasn't just a fascinating creature; it was a companion, a secret confidante. It trusted him. And that trust was a precious, delicate thing he was determined to protect. He found himself thinking less about the journalistic scoop of a lifetime and more about Ingis's well-being. How could he keep it safe? How could he ensure its continued freedom in a world that would undoubtedly seek to cage it?

He began to subtly alter his own habits to accommodate Ingis. He kept his apartment meticulously tidy, knowing Ingis's penchant for shiny objects. He learned to anticipate its visits, leaving out fresh water and new, non-valuable trinkets. He even started carrying a small, soft cloth in his pocket, just in case Ingis needed a gentle rub on its scales.

The cynicism that had defined Gideon Croft for so long was slowly, imperceptibly, eroding. It was being replaced by a quiet wonder, a profound protectiveness, and a sense of purpose he hadn't known he was missing. He was no longer just observing Ingis; he was nurturing a relationship with a creature from myth, a bond forged in shared secrets and the silent understanding between a man and his tiny, fiery dragon. Oakhaven might remain unremarkable to the world, but for Gideon, it was now the most extraordinary place on earth.

Chapter 9

The fragile bond between Gideon and Ingis deepened with each passing day, a silent understanding built on shared secrets and the glint of stolen treasures. Ingis's visits to Gideon's apartment became more frequent, its tiny chirps and playful nudges a welcome counterpoint to the monotonous drone of the *Gazette* office. Gideon, in turn, became more adept at anticipating Ingis's movements, often arriving at the scene of a "theft" just moments after the fact, ready to deploy his carefully crafted diversions and replacement trinkets. He was a one-man clean-up crew for a miniature, fire-breathing kleptomaniac.

But as Gideon grew more comfortable in his role as Ingis's protector, a new, unexpected threat began to emerge, not from Chief Miller's well-meaning but oblivious investigations, but from the unlikeliest of sources: Old Man Fitzwilliam.

Fitzwilliam was Oakhaven's resident eccentric, a fixture on Main Street, usually found perched on a park bench, muttering to himself or haranguing any unfortunate soul who lingered too long. He wore a perpetually stained trench coat, even in summer, and his wild, unkempt white hair seemed to defy gravity. For years, his rants had been harmless background noise – diatribes about alien abductions, government mind control, or the nefarious intentions of the local squirrel population. Gideon had always dismissed him as a harmless crank, occasionally quoting his more outlandish theories in a humorous "Oakhaven Quirks" column.

Lately, however, Fitzwilliam's rants had taken a disturbing turn.

Gideon first heard it while grabbing a lukewarm coffee from the diner. Fitzwilliam was holding court outside, gesticulating wildly at a small group of bewildered tourists. "It's the pixies, I tell ya!" he bellowed, his voice raspy. "Fire-breathing pixies! They're after the shiny things! Seen 'em myself, a flash of green and a puff of smoke! Little devils, they are!"

Gideon nearly choked on his coffee. Fire-breathing pixies. A flash of green. A puff of smoke. Fitzwilliam, in his delusional ramblings, was describing Ingis with unnerving accuracy.

He quickly finished his coffee and retreated, a knot forming in his stomach. He'd always found Fitzwilliam amusing. Now, he found him terrifying. The old man might be crazy, but he was also, accidentally, dangerously close to the truth.

Over the next few days, Fitzwilliam's theories escalated. He started appearing at the scenes of recent "thefts," pointing dramatically at the scorch marks. "See that?" he'd declare to anyone who would listen. "That's dragon breath! Or gnome fire! They're tiny, but they're vicious!" He even started carrying a small, tarnished silver bell, which he would ring erratically, claiming it was a "dragon deterrent."

Gideon, in his *Gazette* articles, continued to dismiss Fitzwilliam's claims with a practiced ease. In a piece about the missing antique compass from the town's maritime museum (another one of Ingis's recent acquisitions, leaving a faint scorch on the display case), Gideon wrote: "While some local residents, such as the venerable Mr. Fitzwilliam, have posited

CHAPTER 9

theories involving 'fire-breathing gnomes,' Chief Miller assures the public that all leads point to a more conventional, albeit elusive, human culprit."

He even added a wry, almost mocking, aside: "Perhaps Mr. Fitzwilliam should consider a career in fantasy literature, where his vivid imagination might find a more suitable outlet than the pages of the *Oakhaven Gazette*."

Publicly, Gideon maintained his cynical, rational facade. Internally, however, he was a coiled spring of nerves. Every time Fitzwilliam opened his mouth, Gideon felt a cold dread. What if someone actually listened? What if someone, even by accident, connected Fitzwilliam's ramblings to the real-world evidence? The scorch marks were undeniable. The missing shiny objects were a fact. All it would take was one person, one curious mind, to put the pieces together.

He found himself subtly trying to steer conversations away from Fitzwilliam. If he saw the old man holding court, Gideon would suddenly remember an urgent errand or a pressing deadline. He even considered trying to reason with Fitzwilliam, but quickly dismissed the idea. You couldn't reason with a conspiracy theorist; you only fueled their fire.

The irony was not lost on him. He, Gideon Croft, who had once yearned for a story that would shake the foundations of belief, was now actively suppressing the most incredible story of his career, all to protect a creature that only a madman (or a journalist with a secret) would believe existed.

One afternoon, Gideon was observing Ingis from his apartment balcony. Ingis was perched on a distant rooftop, meticulously polishing a recently acquired, gleaming silver thimble with its tiny claws. It chirped contentedly, a sound like miniature bells. Just then, from the street below, Gideon heard

Fitzwilliam's voice, amplified by the quiet afternoon.

"They're watching us! The little fire-imps! They love the shine, you see! That's how they find us! Through the shine!"

Ingis, startled by the sudden loud noise, let out a tiny, involuntary sneeze. A pinpoint of flame erupted from its nostrils, briefly illuminating the rooftop before dissipating. It quickly darted away, startled.

Gideon flinched, his heart leaping into his throat. Fitzwilliam hadn't seen it, but he was getting closer. His theories, however outlandish, were becoming a dangerous echo of the truth.

He knew he couldn't silence Fitzwilliam. The old man was too ingrained in the fabric of Oakhaven. But he had to be more careful. He had to redouble his efforts to cover Ingis's tracks, to make the "thefts" seem even more mundane, more easily explained away. The stakes were rising, and the eccentric ramblings of Old Man Fitzwilliam were no longer just amusing; they were a ticking time bomb. Gideon felt the weight of his secret pressing down on him, heavier than ever before.

Chapter 10

The air in Oakhaven had grown thick with whispers. Fitzwilliam's rants, once a source of amusement, now carried a faint, unsettling resonance. People might still roll their eyes, but they also glanced nervously at the scorch marks, at the empty spaces where cherished trinkets once sat. Gideon felt the shift in the town's mood, a subtle undercurrent of unease that threatened to bubble to the surface. He was a tightrope walker, balancing precariously between protecting Ingis and keeping Oakhaven's fragile peace.

His efforts to cover Ingis's tracks became more frantic, more desperate. He replaced a missing silver locket with a polished pewter one, hoping the dim light of Mrs. Gable's parlor would hide the difference. He subtly wiped away a fresh scorch mark from the public library's wooden railing, blaming it on a careless smoker. Each act of deception chipped away at his conscience, but the image of Ingis, small and vulnerable, always won out.

The inevitable escalation came on a crisp autumn morning, heralded by the shrill, insistent ringing of the *Gazette* office phone. Gideon, still half-asleep and nursing a lukewarm coffee, picked it up. It was Mayor Thompson, his voice usually a booming baritone, now a thin, reedy squeak of panic.

"Gideon! You have to get down here! The clock tower! It's... it's gone!"

Gideon's blood ran cold. "What's gone, Mayor?" he asked, a dreadful premonition forming in his gut.

"The key! The golden key! To the clock tower! It was in its velvet display case, right by the entrance, just like always! And now... now it's gone! And there's a mark! A terrible, burnt mark!"

The golden key. Oakhaven's historic clock tower, a symbol of the town's enduring legacy, was wound and maintained by a single, gleaming, ornate golden key, passed down through generations of town elders. It was displayed in a small, glass-fronted case at the base of the tower, a point of pride for tourists and locals alike. It was perhaps the most significant, most *meaningful* shiny object in all of Oakhaven.

Gideon didn't bother with excuses for Brenda. He grabbed his camera and sprinted out the door. This wasn't just another petty theft; this was a public crisis.

The scene at the base of the clock tower was a maelstrom of confusion and concern. Mayor Thompson, his face a mottled red, was pacing frantically. Chief Miller, looking more bewildered than usual, was examining the empty display case, a donut forgotten in his hand. A large crowd had already gathered, their murmurs growing louder, more agitated.

Gideon pushed his way to the front. The display case, usually locked, stood slightly ajar. Inside, the velvet cushion lay empty. And on the cushion, perfectly centered, was a scorch mark. This one was larger than any he'd seen before, a distinct, almost star-shaped burn, as if Ingis had landed directly on it, perhaps in a moment of intense excitement. The faint, familiar scent of burnt sugar and ozone hung heavy in the air.

CHAPTER 10

"No forced entry, Gideon," Chief Miller said, shaking his head. "The glass isn't broken. The lock is intact. It's... it's baffling." His usual dismissive tone was replaced by genuine perplexity.

"Did anyone hear anything?" Gideon asked, trying to sound like a detached reporter, even as his stomach churned.

"Mrs. Gable swore she heard a 'tinkling like tiny bells' around dawn," Mayor Thompson interjected, wringing his hands. "And Mr. Henderson claimed he smelled 'something like a firecracker' from his workshop. But it's just... it's impossible!"

Gideon felt the pressure mounting, a suffocating weight. He knew. He knew exactly what had happened. Ingis, drawn by the irresistible gleam and inherent significance of the key, had taken it. And in its excitement, or perhaps from the effort of carrying such a weighty (for a tiny dragon) prize, it had left a more pronounced mark.

The town was abuzz with theories. "It's a professional thief!" someone shouted. "No, it's a cult!" another cried. And then, inevitably, Fitzwilliam's voice cut through the din, louder and more confident than ever.

"It's the fire-imps, I tell ya! The little dragons! They're getting bolder! They want the gold! They're coming for us all!" He brandished his tarnished silver bell, ringing it furiously.

A ripple of fear, not just amusement, went through the crowd. Fitzwilliam's wild theories, once easily dismissed, now seemed to align disturbingly well with the inexplicable facts. The scorch marks were undeniable. The vanished items were real. And the key to the clock tower was a symbol, a tangible loss that resonated deeply with the townspeople.

Gideon felt a cold dread. This was different. This wasn't just a lost thimble or a missing spatula. This was a direct assault on Oakhaven's sense of security, its very identity. The police were genuinely baffled, and the town was starting to look for answers beyond the mundane.

He saw Chief Miller glance nervously at Fitzwilliam, then at the scorch mark, a flicker of doubt in his eyes. The Chief was a man of logic, but even logic had its limits when faced with the truly inexplicable.

Gideon knew he had to act. He had to find the key. He had to divert suspicion, not just from Ingis, but from the growing, dangerous belief that something supernatural was at play. If the town started to truly believe Fitzwilliam, if they started to hunt for a "fire-imp," Ingis would be in grave danger.

He approached Mayor Thompson, forcing a calm, professional demeanor. "Mayor, I'll write a piece for the *Gazette*. We'll focus on the theft, emphasize the police investigation. Reassure the public."

Thompson nodded, grateful. "Yes, Gideon, please. Something to calm everyone down."

But as Gideon walked away, he knew his article wouldn't be about calming anyone down. It would be about damage control, about buying time. The pressure was immense. He could feel the eyes of the town on him, looking for answers. And he, Gideon Croft, knew the answer. He knew the culprit was a tiny, emerald-scaled dragon named Ingis, currently, no doubt, admiring its new, gleaming golden treasure somewhere high above Oakhaven.

The stakes had never been higher. The clock was ticking, and Gideon knew it wasn't just the town clock. It was the clock on Ingis's secret, counting down to its potential exposure.

Chapter 11

The golden key's disappearance from the clock tower wasn't just a theft; it was a wound to Oakhaven's collective psyche. The town, accustomed to its quiet predictability, now hummed with a nervous energy. The murmurs that had previously been confined to hushed conversations now erupted into open speculation on street corners and in the aisles of the general store. The "local oddities" had escalated into a genuine, unsettling mystery, and the easy explanations were no longer sufficient.

Mayor Thompson, his face still flushed with anxiety, called an emergency town council meeting. The old municipal hall was packed, a rare sight that underscored the gravity of the situation. Citizens, usually content to let local politics drift by, now demanded answers, their voices a rising tide of fear and frustration. Gideon sat in the back, notepad open, but his journalistic detachment was a thin veneer. He felt the tension in the room, the palpable unease that he, and his tiny, golden-key-hoarding dragon, had inadvertently caused.

The debate quickly devolved into a cacophony of theories. Some suggested a sophisticated crime ring, others blamed disgruntled former residents. But the loudest, most persistent voices were those echoing Fitzwilliam. "It's a creature!" one woman cried, her voice trembling. "Something unnatural! It breathes fire!" A ripple of agreement, chillingly widespread, went through the room. Chief Miller, looking more overwhelmed than ever, tried to reassure the crowd, but his words lacked conviction. He too, Gideon noticed, kept glancing at the empty display case, a flicker of doubt in his eyes.

The council eventually voted to increase security measures. Night patrols would be expanded, surveillance cameras (old, grainy ones, but cameras nonetheless) would be installed in public spaces, and a "citizen alert" system was proposed, urging residents to report anything "unusual." It was a desperate attempt to regain control, but to Gideon, it felt like a tightening net.

In the days that followed, Gideon found himself walking a finer line than ever before. His articles for the *Gazette* became a delicate dance of subtle misdirection. He wrote about the "unprecedented security measures," emphasizing the police's commitment to finding a "human culprit." He highlighted the "resilience of Oakhaven's community spirit" in the face of "unexplained incidents," carefully avoiding any language that might legitimize the "monster" or "creature" theories. He framed the thefts as elaborate pranks, perhaps by a bored, highly skilled individual, or even a misguided social experiment. He even managed to slip in a paragraph about the psychological impact of fear, subtly suggesting that the town's imagination might be running wild.

"We need to calm the waters, Gideon," Brenda had said, looking over his latest draft. "People are getting spooked. Keep it grounded."

"Grounded," Gideon repeated, a bitter taste in his mouth. He was grounded, alright. Grounded in the impossible reality of a

CHAPTER 11

tiny dragon and a golden key.

But even as he spun narratives of human mischief and community resilience, Gideon had a second, far more urgent mission: finding Ingis's treasure horde. He knew Ingis wasn't simply eating the shiny objects; it was collecting them. And if he could find where Ingis was stashing its hoard, he might be able to retrieve the key, perhaps even other valuable items, and return them, further deflecting suspicion. More importantly, he could understand Ingis better, and potentially guide its "collecting" habits towards less disruptive targets.

He started by revisiting all the incident locations, not just for new scorch marks, but for any subtle clues. He looked for hidden crevices, abandoned buildings, forgotten nooks and crannies. He spent hours after dark, binoculars in hand, staking out rooftops and old chimneys, hoping to catch a glimpse of Ingis carrying its loot.

He noticed Ingis often flew towards the older, less frequented parts of town – the disused mill on the outskirts, the abandoned train station, the dense woods that bordered Oakhaven to the north. These were places where a tiny, elusive creature could hide a hoard without drawing attention.

He started exploring these areas, carefully, discreetly. He climbed through overgrown paths, peered into darkened windows of derelict buildings, and even ventured into the musty, forgotten corners of the old town library, a place he knew Ingis had visited. He found nothing. No glint of gold, no pile of silver. Ingis was too clever, too small, too good at hiding its treasures.

The search was frustrating, a constant reminder of how little he truly understood about Ingis. He knew its habits, its preferences, its playful nature, but its ultimate sanctuary remained a mystery. He imagined a glittering cave, a secret chamber overflowing with Oakhaven's most cherished, most significant shiny objects, all meticulously arranged by a tiny, discerning dragon.

One evening, after a fruitless search through the old mill, Gideon found himself back at his apartment. He was exhausted, his clothes smudged with dust and cobwebs. He poured himself a glass of water and sat down, staring at the Oakhaven Anomaly Log on his screen. The list of missing items was growing, and with it, the pressure.

He heard a faint scratching at the balcony door. Ingis.

He opened it, and the tiny dragon flew in, landing softly on his desk. In its talons, it held a gleaming, miniature silver locket, one Gideon hadn't seen before. Ingis chirped, then nudged the locket towards him, a silent offering.

Gideon picked up the locket, admiring its intricate engraving. It was beautiful, undeniably precious. And Ingis, in its innocent way, was sharing its newest treasure with him. He looked at the locket, then at the map of Oakhaven on his wall, crisscrossed with lines, a puzzle he desperately needed to solve.

"Where do you keep them all, Ingis?" he whispered, more to himself than to the dragon. "Where's your secret place?"

Ingis tilted its head, its fiery eyes blinking. It let out a soft, bell-like sound, then nudged the locket again, as if urging him to appreciate its beauty.

Gideon sighed, a mix of affection and exasperation. He knew he had to return the locket. He knew he had to keep searching for the horde. But for a moment, he simply held the locket, a tangible link to the impossible, and felt the immense weight of his secret, and his unwavering resolve to protect it. The town might be on edge, but Gideon Croft was now, more than ever, deeply entrenched in Oakhaven's hidden, shimmering truth.

Chapter 12

The increased security measures, the expanded night patrols, and the grainy surveillance cameras did little to deter Ingis. If anything, the heightened tension in Oakhaven seemed to infuse the tiny dragon with a new, almost mischievous audacity. It was as if the collective anxiety of the town was a challenge, an invitation to bolder exploits. Gideon's attempts to find the hoard remained fruitless, and the golden key to the clock tower remained tantalizingly out of reach. The pressure on him was immense, a constant, low thrum beneath the surface of his daily life.

He was in the middle of drafting another carefully worded article for the *Gazette*, this one about the town's new "Neighborhood Watch" initiative (a direct response to the escalating thefts), when Brenda's voice boomed across the newsroom. "Gideon! Mayor Thompson's press conference! You're on!"

Gideon sighed. Public press conferences were usually tedious affairs, filled with platitudes and empty promises. But this one was different. Mayor Thompson was addressing the town's growing unease directly, promising transparency and swift action regarding the "unexplained incidents." It was a high-stakes event, and Gideon knew Ingis, with its uncanny ability to sniff out significant shiny objects, might be drawn to the gathering.

He arrived at the town hall, where a small podium had been set up on the steps. A cluster of reporters, mostly from smaller regional papers, jostled for position. Mayor Thompson, looking harried but determined, stood before them, his dark suit impeccable, a gleaming gold-plated button on his lapel catching the morning sun. Gideon's eyes immediately fixed on it. It was exactly the kind of object Ingis would find irresistible.

He positioned himself strategically, close enough to hear, but with a clear line of sight to the surrounding trees and rooftops. His camera was ready, not for a photo op, but for a quick, discreet shot of a blur of emerald and gold.

Mayor Thompson cleared his throat, adjusting his tie. "My fellow Oakhaven residents," he began, his voice a little shaky, "I understand the concern, the... the unease that has gripped our beloved town. The recent incidents, while perplexing, are being investigated with the utmost diligence..."

As Thompson spoke, Gideon's gaze darted around. He saw a flash of movement from the large oak tree across the street. A tiny, emerald-green shape. Ingis.

The dragon was perched on a high branch, its head cocked, its fiery eyes fixed on the Mayor. More specifically, on the gleaming gold button on his lapel. Gideon's heart hammered against his ribs. *No, Ingis, not now. Not here.*

Thompson continued, oblivious. "...we assure you, every resource is being deployed to apprehend the individual or individuals responsible for these... these acts of petty disruption."

Ingis launched itself from the branch. It was a blur, a streak of green and gold, too fast for the casual observer to truly register. It zipped across the street, a tiny missile aimed directly at the Mayor.

CHAPTER 12

Gideon reacted instinctively. "Mayor!" he shouted, a sudden, desperate cry that cut through Thompson's speech.

Thompson flinched, startled. At that exact moment, Ingis, with a precision that was both terrifying and awe-inspiring, snatched the gold button from his lapel. The dragon didn't even slow down, a faint, almost imperceptible *clink* echoing in the sudden silence as it veered sharply upwards, a tiny puff of smoke escaping its nostrils in a burst of triumphant excitement.

The Mayor blinked, his hand automatically going to his now-empty lapel. The reporters exchanged confused glances. Had Gideon just shouted? What was that flash?

"My... my button!" Thompson stammered, his face paling.

Gideon, ignoring the Mayor, ignored the bewildered reporters. He saw Ingis darting towards the rooftops, a tiny, glittering speck against the sky. He had to follow it. He had to retrieve that button. It was too public, too blatant.

He broke into a run, pushing past a startled cameraman, his eyes fixed on the vanishing dragon. "Excuse me! Urgent call!" he mumbled, trying to sound like a frantic journalist.

But before he could clear the steps, a hand clamped firmly on his arm. It was Chief Miller, his expression a mixture of confusion and suspicion.

"Gideon! What in tarnation was that?" Miller demanded, his grip surprisingly strong. "You just yelled at the Mayor! And what was that flash? Did you see something?"

Gideon struggled, trying to pull away. "Nothing, Chief! Just... just a bee! A really big, shiny bee! And I thought it was going for the Mayor's face! Had to warn him!" He tried to sound convincing, but his voice was strained, his eyes still darting towards the rooftops where Ingis had disappeared.

Miller squinted at him, his gaze lingering on Gideon's frantic, upward glances. "A bee, Gideon? A bee that snatches buttons and leaves a faint smell of... well, it smelled like burnt sugar, now that I think about it." He released Gideon's arm, but his eyes remained narrowed, filled with a new, unsettling suspicion. "You're acting mighty strange, Croft. Mighty strange indeed."

The other reporters, now alerted by the commotion, turned their curious gazes on Gideon. Whispers erupted. "What was that about a bee?" "Croft seems jumpy." "Did he see something?"

Gideon felt their eyes on him, a hundred questions in their stares. He was trapped. Ingis was long gone, a tiny, golden-button-carrying phantom. And he, Gideon Croft, was left standing on the steps of the town hall, the focus of unwanted attention, his cover dangerously blown. The near-miss had turned into a near-exposure, not of Ingis, but of himself. The net was tightening, and Gideon was now firmly caught in its threads.

Chapter 13

The aftermath of the Mayor's button incident left Gideon Croft feeling like a hunted man. Chief Miller's narrowed eyes, the curious glances from other reporters, the buzzing whispers that followed him through the town hall – it all coalesced into a suffocating sense of exposure. His "big bee" excuse had been flimsy at best, and he knew it. The net was tightening, not just around Ingis, but around him. He felt the weight of his secret pressing down, heavier than the golden key Ingis had likely stashed away somewhere.

He spent the next few days in a state of high alert, constantly scanning the skies, checking his apartment for any sign of Ingis, and meticulously reviewing his past articles for any accidental clues he might have left. He even considered trying to subtly discredit Fitzwilliam further, but the old man's wild claims now seemed to hold an uncomfortable grain of truth that resonated with the town's growing unease.

It was during a particularly dull town council meeting, where Gideon was half-listening to a debate about new park benches, that he first saw him. A man in his late thirties, early forties, with an intelligent, intense gaze behind wire-rimmed glasses. He wasn't a local, Gideon could tell immediately. His clothes, though practical, had a subtle academic air, and he carried a small, well-worn leather satchel. He wasn't taking notes on the council proceedings; instead, his eyes were fixed on the scorch mark on the old wooden podium, a faint, almost invisible singe from a past incident Gideon had painstakingly tried to buff out.

The man pulled out a small, specialized camera and took a few discreet photos of the mark, then produced a pair of tweezers and a tiny, sterile vial, carefully collecting a minuscule sample from the charred wood. Gideon's journalistic alarm bells, usually reserved for actual news, screamed. This wasn't a tourist. This was someone with a purpose. And that purpose, Gideon instinctively knew, involved Ingis.

Later that afternoon, back at the *Gazette* office, Brenda called Gideon into her office. Her expression was a mix of curiosity and mild annoyance. "Gideon, there's a Dr. Aris Thorne here to see you. Says he's a naturalist. From out of town. Wants to talk about your articles on the... the Oakhaven incidents."

Gideon's stomach clenched. Thorne. The man from the council meeting. A naturalist. It was worse than he'd imagined. A scientist. Someone who wouldn't be fooled by "big bees" or "disgruntled neighbors."

He walked out to the small, cramped waiting area. Dr. Aris Thorne stood there, impeccably neat despite his field-ready attire. He had a thoughtful, almost scholarly air, and his eyes, when they met Gideon's, were sharp and inquisitive.

"Mr. Croft," Thorne said, extending a hand. His grip was firm, professional. "Dr. Aris Thorne. I hope I'm not interrupting anything vital. I've been following your reporting in the *Gazette* with considerable interest."

Gideon forced a polite smile, his mind racing. "Not at all, Dr. Thorne. Always happy to discuss local news. What can I do for you?"

CHAPTER 13

"Please, Aris is fine," Thorne replied. "Well, to be frank, Mr. Croft, it's not the usual local news that brought me to Oakhaven. It's the... anomalies you've been reporting on. The missing shiny objects. And, more specifically, the scorch marks."

Gideon's smile tightened. "The scorch marks? Chief Miller believes those are mostly accidental, or perhaps from... less careful individuals."

Thorne chuckled softly, a sound devoid of humor. "Chief Miller's theories, while admirably pragmatic, don't quite align with the scientific evidence, Mr. Croft. These aren't cigarette burns. They're too precise. Too unique. I've been tracking similar phenomena online, in various science forums and niche communities. The chemical composition of the residue, the heat signature... it's unlike anything known."

He paused, his gaze fixed on Gideon. "Your articles, Mr. Croft, particularly your early pieces on Mrs. Gable's thimbles and Mr. Henderson's watch, were among the first to detail these specific characteristics. You've been remarkably observant. And your recent piece on the clock tower key... that was the clincher. A significant, high-profile incident with a very distinct mark."

Gideon felt a cold dread spread through him. Thorne wasn't just a curious amateur; he was a serious scientist, and he had been meticulously following Gideon's own breadcrumbs. Every subtle detail Gideon had included, every precise description of a scorch mark, was now being used against him, against Ingis.

"So, you're here to... investigate?" Gideon asked, trying to keep his voice neutral.

"Precisely," Thorne confirmed, a flicker of excitement in his eyes. "I believe we're dealing with an unknown phenomenon, perhaps even a new species. The energy output required for these scorch marks, the selective nature of the 'thefts' for shiny, often valuable objects... it's fascinating. And quite unlike anything I've encountered in my career as a naturalist."

He leaned forward slightly, his voice dropping to a more confidential tone. "I've already taken some preliminary samples from the clock tower. The residue is... extraordinary. I'd be very interested, Mr. Croft, if you could share any further observations you've made. As the local journalist, you've had unparalleled access to these incidents. Perhaps you've noticed patterns, or even... glimpses of the perpetrator, however fleeting?"

Gideon's mind raced. Thorne wasn't just asking questions; he was *probing*. He wasn't falling for the "prankster" narrative. He was looking for a creature. A new species. And Gideon knew, with a certainty that chilled him to the bone, that if Thorne found Ingis, the dragon's secret, and its freedom, would be irrevocably lost. This wasn't Chief Miller's amiable dismissal; this was the sharp, intelligent, relentless pursuit of scientific discovery. And it was a far greater threat.

"I... I've just been reporting the facts, Dr. Thorne," Gideon stammered, trying to regain his composure. "No glimpses of anything beyond the ordinary, I assure you. Just... unusual circumstances."

Thorne's eyes seemed to twinkle behind his glasses. "Of course, Mr. Croft. Just the facts. But sometimes, the facts lead to extraordinary conclusions. I look forward to collaborating with you on this. Perhaps together, we can unravel Oakhaven's peculiar mystery."

He offered another polite smile, but Gideon saw the determination in his gaze. Thorne wasn't leaving. He was here to stay. And he was going to find Ingis. Gideon felt a cold knot of fear in his stomach. His secret, Ingis's life, now depended on his ability to outwit a sharp, scientifically-minded naturalist. The game had just gotten infinitely more dangerous.

Chapter 14

The encounter with Dr. Aris Thorne had left Gideon Croft with a cold, hard knot of fear in his gut. Chief Miller was one thing – easily misled, focused on the mundane. But Thorne was different. Thorne was a scientist, driven by intellectual curiosity and equipped with the tools to dissect the impossible. He wouldn't be satisfied with vague explanations or convenient coincidences. He would dig, he would analyze, and eventually, he would find Ingis.

After Thorne had left the *Gazette* office, Gideon had rushed home, his mind racing. He found Ingis perched on his bookshelf, meticulously arranging a small collection of shiny thimbles and a particularly lustrous antique button. Gideon scooped the tiny dragon up, holding it gently in his cupped hands.

"Ingis," he whispered, holding his phone up to show a photo of Dr. Thorne. "This man. He's dangerous. He knows about the scorch marks. He's looking for you."

Ingis chirped, its fiery eyes blinking, seemingly oblivious to the gravity of Gideon's words. It nudged the phone screen with its snout, then let out a tiny, playful puff of smoke.

"No, Ingis," Gideon insisted, trying to convey the urgency. "He's a scientist. He'll want to study you. He'll want to capture you." He then tried a different tactic. "Show me your hoard,

Ingis. The golden key. If I can get it back, maybe he'll leave."

He set Ingis down on the floor, gesturing vaguely towards the window, hoping the dragon would lead him to its secret stash. Ingis looked at him, then let out a soft, bell-like sound, before darting across the room to bat playfully at a sunbeam dancing on the wall. It was clear: Ingis, in its innocent, instinct-driven world, had no concept of "danger" or "hiding place" in the human sense. It simply collected, and it trusted Gideon. The hoard, and the golden key, remained a secret.

Frustration surged through Gideon, quickly followed by a renewed sense of resolve. He couldn't rely on Ingis to protect itself. He had to be smarter, more cunning. He had to throw Thorne off the scent.

The next morning, Gideon approached Dr. Thorne at the local coffee shop, where the naturalist was meticulously examining a sample of charred wood under a portable microscope.

"Dr. Thorne," Gideon began, trying to sound casual, "I've been thinking about our conversation yesterday. About the... anomalies."

Thorne looked up, his eyes sharp. "Oh? And have you had any epiphanies, Mr. Croft?"

"Perhaps," Gideon said, leaning in conspiratorially, lowering his voice. "You mentioned the unique properties of the scorch marks. The chemical composition. I was thinking... have you considered local flora?"

Thorne raised an eyebrow. "Local flora?"

"Yes," Gideon pressed, warming to his fabricated narrative. "Oakhaven is known for its surprisingly diverse ecosystem. And there's a particular species of fungi, *Luminosa carbonis*, that grows in the older, damp parts of town. It's bioluminescent, but also, under certain atmospheric conditions, it's known to produce a highly reactive carbon compound. A kind of... spontaneous combustion, if you will. Very rare, of course."

Thorne's expression remained skeptical, but a flicker of scientific curiosity entered his eyes. "Spontaneous combustion from a fungus? That's... an interesting hypothesis, Mr. Croft. Do you have any samples of this *Luminosa carbonis*?"

"Not on me, unfortunately," Gideon replied smoothly. "It's quite elusive. But I could perhaps point you towards some areas where it's been sighted. Near the old mill, for instance. Or the abandoned train tracks. Very damp, very overgrown." He was steering Thorne towards places Ingis *didn't* frequent, or at least, didn't use as primary perches.

Thorne made a note in a small, leather-bound journal. "Intriguing. I'll certainly investigate. Though the scorch marks suggest a more direct, localized heat source than a general atmospheric reaction."

Gideon pressed on, undeterred. "Or, alternatively," he continued, "have you considered the town's antiquated plumbing system? There are some very old, corroded pipes running beneath Oakhaven. Some speculate about obscure chemical reactions, perhaps involving trace minerals in the water, creating highly corrosive, even exothermic, byproducts that could surface as... small, localized burns."

Thorne paused, a thoughtful frown on his face. "Exothermic reactions in municipal pipes? That's... a stretch, Mr. Croft. The energy output would be immense, and the pattern of the marks doesn't suggest a slow seep or corrosion." He tapped his pen against his journal. "Still, a novel idea. I'll make a note of it."

Gideon felt a glimmer of hope. Thorne wasn't buying it outright, but he wasn't dismissing it completely either. He was a scientist; he was open to possibilities, however outlandish.

CHAPTER 14

"And then there's the squirrels," Gideon added, lowering his voice even further. "Oakhaven has a particularly robust squirrel population. Highly energetic. Some locals swear they've seen them with static electricity building up, especially on dry days. And they do have a peculiar fondness for shiny objects, don't they? Perhaps a new, highly charged subspecies, prone to... accidental discharges?"

Thorne actually cracked a small smile at this, a rare display of amusement. "A highly energetic, static-prone squirrel with a penchant for shiny objects? Mr. Croft, your imagination is certainly... vivid." He closed his journal. "While I appreciate your creative hypotheses, I must confess, the evidence I've gathered so far points to something far more... biologically complex than a super-charged rodent or a combusting fungus."

Gideon's heart sank. Thorne was skeptical, but he was also clearly intrigued by the sheer *uniqueness* of the phenomena. His scientific curiosity was piqued, not satisfied. He was a bloodhound, and Gideon's false trails, while momentarily distracting, weren't enough to throw him off the scent entirely.

"Nevertheless," Thorne continued, rising from his seat, "I thank you for your suggestions, Mr. Croft. They provide... interesting avenues for consideration. I'll be conducting more field research around town. Perhaps we'll cross paths again."

As Thorne walked away, Gideon watched him, a cold dread returning. He had tried. He had thrown out every plausible-sounding, yet ultimately false, lead he could concoct. Thorne hadn't swallowed them whole, but he hadn't dismissed them either. He was still in Oakhaven, still investigating, still looking for the truth. And Gideon knew, with a chilling certainty, that the truth, in this case, was a tiny, emerald-scaled dragon named Ingis. The misdirection had bought him some time, but it wouldn't last forever. The game of cat and mouse had just begun, and Gideon felt very much like the mouse.

Chapter 15

Oakhaven's annual Summer Fair was usually a highlight of the season, a brief, saccharine burst of collective joy before the long, sleepy slide into autumn. For Gideon Croft, it had always been an assignment to be endured: cover the opening ceremonies, snap photos of grinning children on carousel horses, write a bland piece about corn dogs and community spirit. This year, however, the fair was less a charming local event and more a chaotic, glittering minefield.

The moment Gideon saw the first flicker of the fairgrounds from his apartment balcony, a familiar knot of dread tightened in his stomach. Construction crews had spent the better part of the week erecting the temporary cityscape of canvas tents, gleaming rides, and towering light fixtures in the town's large, open field. Now, as dusk settled, the field was alive with an incandescent glow. Thousands of tiny, naked bulbs strung along wires pulsed and flashed. Spin-and-vomit rides adorned with chrome and mirrors whirred and spun, catching the last rays of sun in blinding flashes. Prize booths, draped in shimmering tinsel and stocked with glittering plastic trophies, beckoned with their impossible odds.

It was a veritable supernova of shine. And Gideon knew, with a terrifying certainty, that Ingis would find it utterly irresistible.

His premonition proved correct almost immediately. As the fair officially opened with a modest burst of fireworks – a surprisingly small display that Gideon, for once, was grateful for – he saw Ingis. The tiny dragon, a fleeting emerald streak, darted from the familiar oak tree in the town square, drawn like a moth to the overwhelming, multi-faceted allure of the fairgrounds.

Gideon scrambled, grabbing his camera, ostensibly to "cover the opening night," but his real mission was clear: keep Ingis hidden. He waded into the surging river of people, a human shield against potential disaster. The fair was a sensory assault. The air vibrated with the competing thrum of generators, the shrieks of children on spinning rides, the tinny, distorted music of carousels and shooting galleries. The smell of fried dough, popcorn, and syrupy sweet drinks mingled with the faint, metallic tang of the rides. And everywhere, a dazzling, overwhelming explosion of light and glitter.

He spotted Ingis first near the 'Ring Toss' game, perched precariously on a string of flashing LED lights. Its tiny head was tilted, its fiery eyes wide with what could only be described as pure, unadulterated awe. The sheer concentration of shiny objects – cheap plastic rings, polished glass bottles, the shimmering prize ribbons hanging from the tent ceiling – was intoxicating to the dragon. A small, involuntary puff of smoke escaped its nostrils, quickly lost in the general haze of fairground fumes.

Gideon moved in, trying to block the dragon from casual view. He pretended to be intensely interested in the game, feigning exasperation at his inability to land a ring. He kept one eye on Ingis, the other on the surging crowd. Every time someone got too close, Gideon would subtly shift, or cough loudly, or "accidentally" bump into them, diverting their attention.

His heart pounded. The noise was a particular challenge. Ingis, while not outwardly sensitive, seemed to react to sudden, loud sounds with those dreaded fiery sneezes. The booming speakers, the sudden clang of a dropped prize, the piercing scream from the 'Gravitron' – each sound was a potential eruption. Gideon found himself flinching every few minutes, bracing for the tell-tale glow, only to find it hadn't materialized. Yet.

The real trouble started near the 'Whirlwind' ride. Its gleaming chrome arms spun wildly, catching the light in a dizzying display. Ingis, mesmerized, flew too close, its small form a fleeting emerald flash against the backdrop of spinning metal. A few people gasped, pointing. "Did you see that?" one boy exclaimed, wide-eyed. "A green bird!"

Gideon, already moving, pretended to stumble, dropping his camera with a loud clatter. The noise drew attention, and when people looked back at the ride, Ingis was gone, having darted away into the cover of a concession stand tent. Gideon quickly retrieved his camera, muttering apologies and feigning embarrassment, his face flushed not from shame, but from sheer terror.

He followed Ingis to the prize booth, a luminous cave of cheap treasures. Here, the dragon was in its element. It was darting between rows of oversized plush toys, its eyes gleaming as it contemplated the shiny, foil-wrapped candy bars and the glittering plastic keychains. A particularly gaudy, mirror-studded disco ball hanging near the ceiling seemed to captivate it.

Gideon saw his chance. He pulled out a handful of crinkled aluminum foil from his pocket – his usual Ingis lure – and quietly tossed a piece behind a stack of giant stuffed animals. Ingis immediately abandoned its contemplation of the disco ball and zipped towards the foil, its tiny chirrup a sound of pure delight. Gideon quickly bought a ridiculously oversized teddy bear, using it as a screen to block Ingis from view as the dragon investigated the foil.

The effort was exhausting. The crowds were relentless, a constant, shifting sea of legs and torsos. The noise was a pounding headache. The flashing lights made his eyes ache. And every single glint, every shimmer from a dropped coin or a child's toy, was a potential magnet for Ingis. He felt like a desperate parent trying to keep a toddler from touching everything in a china shop, only his toddler could fly and accidentally set things on fire.

He had another near-miss at the 'Dunk Tank.' The water was constantly agitated, catching the lights in dazzling splashes. Ingis, drawn by the chaotic sparkle, flew directly over the tank. A child, having just hit the target, let out a triumphant shriek as the volunteer plunged into the water. The sudden noise made Ingis flinch. A tiny, almost invisible spark ignited above the water for a split second before vanishing. No one else seemed to notice, thankfully, but Gideon felt a fresh wave of nausea.

He tried to guide Ingis away from the most crowded and brightest areas, subtly herding it towards the quieter edges of the fairgrounds, towards the less interesting food stalls or the exit gates. He found himself improvising, inventing distractions on the fly. He'd "accidentally" spill his drink, causing a commotion. He'd point dramatically at nothing in particular, shouting, "Look! A comet!" to draw eyes away from a fleeting green blur.

The psychological toll was immense. He was constantly

CHAPTER 15

on edge, his senses overloaded. Every laugh, every scream, every sudden movement was a threat. His journalistic skills, once focused on observation and analysis, were now honed for evasion and subterfess. He was a master of distraction, a professional obfuscator. But for how long?

As the night wore on, the fairgrounds grew even more chaotic. The music got louder, the crowds thicker. Ingis, despite its brief moments of being startled, seemed to be thriving in the sensory overload, its curiosity boundless. It briefly perched on the edge of a candy apple, fascinated by the sugary glaze, then zipped off to investigate the gleaming brass casing of a popcorn machine.

Gideon felt a desperate weariness settle over him. He was losing control. The fair was too big, too bright, too loud. He couldn't possibly account for every one of Ingis's impulsive movements, every accidental fiery sneeze. The golden key of the clock tower was one thing; a public exposure at the Oakhaven Summer Fair was another entirely. It would shatter the town's illusions, ignite widespread panic, and inevitably lead to a hunt for Ingis that Gideon knew he couldn't stop alone.

He spotted Chief Miller near the Ferris wheel, casually chatting with a vendor, his eyes scanning the crowd. Gideon quickly ducked behind a game booth, his heart pounding. The Chief wasn't just observing the crowds; he was looking for something specific, something unusual.

Gideon knew he couldn't stay. He had to get Ingis out of here. But how? The fair was a labyrinth of lights and noise, and Ingis, in its glittering paradise, seemed disinclined to leave. Gideon took a deep breath, steeling himself. He had to find a way to lure Ingis out, safely and discreetly, before the chaos of the fair consumed them both. The night was still young, and the biggest, most dangerous test of his guardianship was just beginning.

Chapter 16

The fairgrounds pulsed with a life of its own, a glittering, roaring beast that swallowed sounds and cast long, distorted shadows. Gideon, trapped within its dazzling maw, felt his energy draining, his frantic efforts to shadow Ingis becoming less precise, more desperate. He'd lost sight of Chief Miller, but the knowledge that the Chief was somewhere in the crowd, looking for "something unusual," sent constant shivers down his spine.

Ingis, however, was undeterred by Gideon's mounting anxiety. If anything, the chaos of the fair seemed to fuel its exuberance. It zipped through the air, a tiny, emerald bullet of insatiable curiosity, from the dizzying lights of the Ferris wheel to the shimmering prizes of the midway games. Gideon followed, weaving through families, ducking under stretched wires, his eyes constantly scanning for the tell-tale glint of his charge.

He found Ingis hovering near the 'Balloon Pop' game, its attention fixed on a particularly garish, silver-foil prize ribbon hanging from the tent. The ribbon, reflecting the chaotic kaleidoscope of fairground lights, shimmered with an almost hypnotic allure. The stall owner, a burly man with a booming voice, was loudly coaxing customers, his gaze fixed on his targets, not the air above him.

"Step right up! Three darts for five dollars! Pop a balloon, win a prize!" the owner bellowed.

Ingis, completely oblivious to the human interaction, darted forward. It was a swift, silent move, almost invisible against the backdrop of flashing lights. With an expert flick of its tiny talons, the dragon snatched the gleaming silver ribbon.

The stall owner, mid-sentence, paused. He blinked, a bewildered expression crossing his face. The ribbon was gone. And on the painted wooden frame of the stall, precisely where the ribbon had hung, was a small, star-shaped scorch mark, the wood faintly smoking.

A few fairgoers, waiting their turn, noticed. A young couple, their arms laden with oversized stuffed animals, pointed. "Hey! What was that?" the man exclaimed, his eyes wide.

Before Gideon could react, Ingis, emboldened by its successful snatch, performed a quick, celebratory loop in the air above the stall. In its excitement, a small, involuntary burst of flame, no bigger than a flicker, erupted from its nostrils, momentarily illuminating its emerald scales before vanishing. It was gone in an instant, a blink-and-you-miss-it phenomenon.

The couple, and a few others standing nearby, gasped. The woman clutched her boyfriend's arm. "Did you see that? A flash of... fire?"

"Must be a trick of the lights," the boyfriend mumbled, trying to sound reassuring. "Or a faulty wire. This whole place is held together with duct tape and prayers." He laughed nervously.

The stall owner, still reeling from the missing ribbon and the scorch mark, quickly joined in. "Yeah, yeah! Just a short circuit! Happens all the time with these old lights! Nothing to worry about folks, step right up, pop a balloon!" He immediately grabbed another ribbon, a less shiny red one, and hastily tied it to the spot, trying to distract from the lingering smell of ozone.

Gideon, who had frozen, watching the terrifying scene unfold, exhaled slowly. It had been a near-panic. A few startled fairgoers, yes, but not widespread alarm. The fair's inherent chaos and the public's willingness to dismiss anomalies as mechanical failures or tricks of light had worked in Ingis's favor.

He quickly approached the stall, feigning interest in the game. He pulled out his wallet, pretending to buy darts, while subtly examining the scorch mark. It was undeniable. Ingis's signature. He made a mental note to return later, perhaps with his cleaning kit.

He glanced at the young couple. They were still whispering, their eyes occasionally darting back to the stall. But the thrill of the fair, the promise of prizes, was quickly reasserting itself. They shrugged, laughed, and moved on, drawn by the vibrant sounds of the Ferris wheel.

Gideon felt a mix of profound relief and renewed dread. Ingis had gotten away with it, thanks to the sensory overload of the fair. But the incident was a stark reminder of the knife-edge he was walking. The dragon was becoming bolder, its excitement leading to more frequent, and more noticeable, fiery sneezes. And each time, the risk of full exposure grew exponentially.

He saw Ingis, a tiny, glittering speck, disappearing into the maze of rides and tents, the silver ribbon clutched proudly in its talons. Gideon sighed. The night was far from over, and with Ingis's insatiable desire for shine, another accidental revelation was only a sudden loud noise, or a particularly dazzling prize, away. He had to find a way to extract Ingis from this glittering trap, and soon.

Chapter 17

The Oakhaven Summer Fair finally packed up its glittering chaos, leaving behind nothing but trampled grass, discarded candy wrappers, and a lingering scent of fried dough and ozone. For Gideon, the fair had been a terrifying dance on a razor's edge, a constant barrage of near-exposures for Ingis. The incident with the prize ribbon had been a stark reminder that Oakhaven's collective dismissal of anomalies was a fragile defense. And now, the town was quieter, but the undercurrent of unease, far from dissipating, had deepened.

Gideon was back at his desk, staring at the blank screen, trying to formulate a "feel-good" wrap-up article about the fair. His phone rang. It was Chief Miller. Gideon's stomach tightened. Miller rarely called him directly, usually relying on Brenda.

"Croft? You got a minute? Come on down to the station." Miller's voice was uncharacteristically sober, devoid of his usual cheerful resignation.

Gideon arrived at the small, brick police station, his heart pounding. Chief Miller sat behind his cluttered desk, not eating a donut for once. He looked tired, his brow furrowed with genuine concern. He waved Gideon to the chair opposite him.

"This isn't about that Mayor's button incident, Gideon,"

CHAPTER 17

Miller began, surprising Gideon with his directness. "Well, not directly. But it's all connected, isn't it?"

Gideon swallowed. "Connected, Chief? To what?"

Miller leaned back, his chair groaning. "Look, Gideon, I'm a pragmatic man. Always have been. I believe in logical explanations, in tangible evidence. Kids. Pranksters. Misplaced items. That's my bread and butter. But lately... lately, things just aren't adding up."

He picked up a file, a slim folder that Gideon suspected was his growing "Oakhaven Anomaly Log." "Mrs. Gable's thimbles. Mr. Henderson's watch. Sal's spatula. The clock tower key. And now, Mrs. Davison's prized silver brooch that vanished from her mantelpiece last night, leaving a scorch mark the size of a dime." Miller slowly shook his head. "No forced entry, Gideon. Every single time. And these scorch marks... they're all identical. Tiny. Precise. And always that faint smell. Like burnt something or other."

He met Gideon's gaze, his eyes weary but surprisingly sharp. "You've been to all these scenes, Gideon. You're the news guy. You're the one who's actually *looked* at these things, written about them. My officers, bless their hearts, they just want to file reports and go home. But you... you see things. You connect dots."

Gideon felt a surge of cold fear mixed with a strange, almost paternal pride. Miller was seeing the pattern. He was closer than ever.

"I'm running out of logical explanations, Gideon," Miller admitted, his voice a low rumble. "Folks are talking. Fitzwilliam, he's not helping, but he's not entirely wrong anymore, either. People are scared. They're starting to believe in... in things that don't exist." He leaned forward, his elbows on the desk. "So,

I'm asking you, Gideon. Off the record. Man to man. You've been following these incidents closer than anyone. What do *you* think is going on?"

The direct question hit Gideon like a physical blow. Miller trusted him. He was appealing to Gideon's investigative skills, his journalistic mind. This was the moment of truth. He could tell him. He could reveal Ingis. But then, what? Capture? Study? The very thought sent a shiver down his spine.

"Chief," Gideon began, choosing his words carefully, "it's... it's certainly perplexing. The pattern is undeniable, I agree." He paused, desperately searching for a convincing, yet utterly false, explanation. "My working theory, and it's just a theory, mind you, is that we're dealing with a highly sophisticated individual. Someone with intimate knowledge of Oakhaven, its residents' habits, its security weaknesses. A master illusionist, perhaps."

Miller raised an eyebrow. "An illusionist who leaves scorch marks and smells like burnt sugar?"

"Perhaps part of their act," Gideon pushed, grasping at straws. "Or a chemical byproduct of their tools. Something designed to mislead, to create a sense of the inexplicable. To make us look for something that isn't there."

Miller sat back, his gaze unblinking. He didn't look convinced, but he didn't look entirely dismissive either. "A very... elaborate prank, Gideon. For a few thimbles and a spatula."

"Perhaps they enjoy the challenge, Chief," Gideon replied, feeling the words taste like ash in his mouth. "Or they're building to something. A bigger statement. Maybe they're just trying to prove how vulnerable Oakhaven is."

Miller sighed, running a hand over his face. "Maybe. Or maybe I'm just getting old and seeing things. But Gideon, something about this... it feels different. It doesn't feel human."

CHAPTER 17

He looked at Gideon again, a silent plea in his eyes. "You're a good reporter, Gideon. Keep your eyes open. If you see anything, anything at all, you come to me first. No questions asked."

Gideon nodded, a lump in his throat. He had just lied to Chief Miller, to a man who genuinely trusted him. The guilt was immediate, a heavy stone in his chest. But the image of Ingis, small and vulnerable, chirping playfully in his apartment, overshadowed the guilt. He had to protect it. At any cost.

Chapter 18

The conversation with Chief Miller gnawed at Gideon. The Chief's admission of baffling perplexity, his reluctant step away from pure logic, and his direct appeal to Gideon's investigative skills had struck a nerve. Gideon Croft, the cynical journalist, had always prided himself on seeking the truth, on exposing what lay hidden. Now, he was actively obscuring it, weaving webs of misdirection, and deceiving a man who genuinely trusted him.

Every time he sat down to write an article for the *Gazette*, the journalistic dilemma screamed louder in his head. His fingers hovered over the keyboard, but the words felt tainted. He was supposed to inform, to uncover. Instead, he was fabricating, misleading, and complicit in a secret that was slowly but surely eroding Oakhaven's sense of reality.

He thought of his journalism school professors, their impassioned lectures on integrity, on the sacred duty to report, on being the voice of truth. He remembered the thrill of his early investigative pieces, the moral clarity of pursuing a story no matter where it led. That Gideon Croft would have broken the story of Ingis the moment he saw the iridescent scale. That Gideon Croft would be pounding on Brenda's door, demanding a front-page exposé.

CHAPTER 18

But that Gideon Croft felt like a distant memory, replaced by a guardian, a silent protector. His burgeoning desire to protect Ingis, this impossible, beautiful, mischievous creature, now outweighed his professional obligations. It wasn't a conscious choice he'd made; it was an innate, undeniable pull, a responsibility that had slowly, irrevocably, taken root in his soul.

He had another brief, tense encounter with Miller a few days later, while covering a bake sale (the irony was not lost on him). Miller pulled him aside, a worried frown on his face. "Anything new on your 'master illusionist,' Gideon?" he asked, his tone still professional, but with an underlying weariness. "Mrs. Finch found another scorch mark in the library, near the antique globe. And her shiny little magnifying glass is gone."

Gideon felt a fresh wave of panic. Ingis was getting bolder, its taste for meaningful items leading it to more public, more obvious targets. He quickly composed himself, offering Miller another vague, unhelpful theory. "Perhaps the 'illusionist' is escalating, Chief. Trying to provoke a response. A bigger statement, as I suggested." He tried to sound confident, but he could feel the flush rising in his cheeks.

Miller just sighed, shaking his head. "Provoking a response, huh? Well, he's certainly doing that. Keep me in the loop, Gideon. Any lead, no matter how small."

As Miller walked away, Gideon felt a sharp pang of guilt. The Chief was clearly struggling, genuinely baffled, and Gideon was actively hindering his investigation. He was lying, not just to Miller, but to the entire town. He was undermining his own profession, abandoning the very principles he once held dear.

He sought solace in Ingis's presence. The tiny dragon, oblivious to the moral quandaries it caused, would often visit his apartment, sometimes leaving a newly acquired trinket – a gleaming silver button, a miniature ornate key – on his desk. Gideon would sit there, staring at the glittering object, then at the empty space on his professional conscience.

He knew he couldn't maintain this deception indefinitely. The incidents were piling up, the evidence of something extraordinary was becoming too overwhelming. Sooner or later, someone would put the pieces together, and then his journalistic integrity, and Ingis's freedom, would both be on the line. He was buying time, but the cost was increasingly heavy. Every white lie, every deflected question, felt like a betrayal. But then, he'd remember Ingis's bright, intelligent eyes, its playful chirps, its innocent desire for shine, and the choice, however difficult, seemed clear. He would protect his tiny dragon, even if it meant sacrificing the journalist he once was.

Chapter 19

The precarious balance Gideon maintained between protecting Ingis and deceiving Oakhaven was about to be irrevocably shattered, not by Chief Miller's growing suspicion, but by the cold, scientific precision of Dr. Aris Thorne. Gideon's attempts at misdirection, his fabricated tales of bioluminescent fungi and super-charged squirrels, had bought him some time, but they had not deterred the naturalist.

A few weeks after their initial meeting, Gideon received an email from Thorne. The subject line read: "Preliminary Findings - Oakhaven Anomaly." Gideon's heart sank. He opened the email with trembling fingers.

The email contained a link to a digital pre-print of a paper titled: "Unidentified Combustion Residue and Selective Object Displacements in a Rural North American Township: A Preliminary Biogeochemical Analysis." It was published in a niche, online regional science journal, *The Journal of Unexplained Natural Phenomena*.

Gideon clicked the link, his dread mounting. The report was meticulously detailed, filled with scientific jargon Gideon barely understood, but the implications were horrifyingly clear. Thorne had analyzed the samples from the scorch marks – the clock tower, the diner counter, Mrs. Davison's mantelpiece. He had used advanced spectroscopic analysis, gas chromatography, and electron microscopy.

The report detailed the unique chemical composition of the residue: trace elements of rare earth metals, carbon nanoparticles with an unusual crystalline structure, and residual compounds consistent with a rapid, intense, but highly localized heat source, unlike any known combustion. It concluded, with careful scientific language, that the marks were not from conventional sources like cigarettes, lighters, or even electrical faults.

Then came the kicker. The report stated: "The consistent association of these unique combustion residues with the selective displacement of metallic, highly reflective, and often anecdotally 'cherished' objects, alongside sporadic auditory (e.g., 'tinkling sounds') and olfactory (e.g., 'burnt sugar,' 'ozone') phenomena, suggests the involvement of a hitherto unidentified biological agent or atmospheric phenomenon."

Thorne hadn't mentioned "dragon." He hadn't said "creature" outright. But "unidentified biological agent" was close enough to send a chill down Gideon's spine. The language was academic, dry, yet it painted a picture that was far more concrete than Chief Miller's "prankster" theories or Fitzwilliam's "fire-imps."

Gideon felt a surge of despair. Thorne's report, though scientific and cautious, was precisely the kind of legitimate, documented evidence that would fuel the "creature" narrative. It lent credibility to Fitzwilliam's ramblings, inadvertently turning the town's resident conspiracy theorist into a prophet. People might dismiss Fitzwilliam, but they couldn't dismiss a peer-reviewed scientific paper.

He scrolled through the comments section below the report.

CHAPTER 19

They were already pouring in. "Amazing work, Dr. Thorne!" "This validates what so many have been saying for years!" "Could it be a new form of cryptid?" "The Oakhaven Fiery Fairy!"

Gideon slammed his laptop shut. The internet was a dangerous place. Thorne, in his detached pursuit of scientific truth, had unwittingly given legitimacy to the very fears Gideon had worked so hard to suppress. The small, sleepy town of Oakhaven, which had dismissed its missing thimbles as mere oddities, was now being presented with scientific proof that something truly inexplicable was afoot.

He imagined the headlines in the larger regional papers, once they picked up on Thorne's report. "Scientist Confirms Unidentified Phenomenon in Oakhaven!" "Biological Agent Behind Local Thefts!" It was a short leap from "biological agent" to "monster."

Gideon felt the walls closing in. Thorne's scientific pursuit, meant to shed light, was inadvertently throwing a dangerous spotlight directly onto Ingis. The "creature" narrative, once confined to Fitzwilliam's eccentric corner, was now being given a scientific foundation. The town council's debates about security measures would intensify. Chief Miller's baffled pursuit would gain a new, desperate focus. And the hunter, Silas Blackwood, would no doubt be emboldened.

Gideon looked out his window at the quiet Oakhaven street. The lights of the town were starting to come on. Somewhere out there, Ingis was probably flying, perhaps admiring a newly acquired piece of shine. And somewhere else, Dr. Thorne was likely already planning his next research trip, blissfully unaware of the storm he was brewing. Gideon knew he had to act fast. The time for subtle misdirection was over. The game had just gotten real.

Chapter 20

The digital hum of Dr. Aris Thorne's report had not just echoed through the Oakhaven Gazette office; it had reverberated through every home in town. The discreet link, shared by Gideon, had been swiftly discovered, copied, and spread like wildfire across Oakhaven's small online community forums and local social media groups. No longer were the strange incidents just "local oddities" or the ramblings of old Fitzwilliam. Now, they were legitimate, scientifically validated anomalies. The term "unidentified biological agent" became the chilling new mantra, replacing "prankster" and "squirrel."

Fear, a raw, primal emotion Oakhaven had rarely encountered, now gripped the town. Doors were locked earlier. Children were kept indoors after dusk. Neighborhood watch groups, once a quaint, symbolic gesture, transformed into earnest, patrolling units, their flashlights piercing the night. Every fleeting shadow, every unexplained sound, was scrutinized. The very fabric of Oakhaven's peaceful, predictable existence had been irrevocably torn.

Mayor Thompson, his face etched with deeper lines of worry than usual, called another emergency town hall meeting. This time, there was no need to coax attendance. The Oakhaven Municipal Hall, usually only half-filled for even the most contentious debates, was overflowing. The standing-room-only crowd spilled out onto the front steps, a silent, tense sea of faces illuminated by the flickering streetlights. Inside, the air was thick with nervous energy, the collective anxiety almost palpable.

Gideon Croft sat near the back, an uncomfortable knot of dread tightening in his stomach. He was no longer just a reporter observing a story; he was a participant, an unwilling accomplice to the panic, the keeper of the very secret that now threatened to unravel everything. He clutched his notepad, but his hand trembled.

Mayor Thompson, a bead of sweat tracing a path down his temple despite the cool autumn evening, stepped up to the podium. His usual booming voice was strained. "My fellow Oakhavenites," he began, attempting to inject a semblance of calm into the agitated crowd, "I understand your concerns. The recent... incidents, particularly the disappearance of the clock tower key, and now Dr. Thorne's report, have naturally caused... distress."

A murmur rippled through the hall. Someone shouted, "Distress? We're terrified, Mayor!"

Thompson raised a placating hand. "We are addressing this. Chief Miller and his department are working tirelessly. We are in consultation with... with external experts." He avoided mentioning "Dr. Thorne" directly, as if the name itself might conjure the very "agent" they feared.

Just then, Old Man Fitzwilliam, who had somehow managed to elbow his way to the front row, suddenly leaped onto a chair. His trench coat flapped around him like a dark banner, and his wild white hair seemed to crackle with an unnatural energy. "He ain't telling ya the truth!" Fitzwilliam shrieked, his voice raw, surprisingly powerful. "It's the fire-imps! The little dragons! I told ya! They're here! They love the shine, they feed on it! And now they've got a taste for the important things! The key! They're getting stronger!"

A wave of contradictory reactions swept through the crowd. Some scoffed, muttering "Crazy old fool." But others, a significant number, listened with wide, horrified eyes. Fitzwilliam, once a pariah, was now a prophet, his bizarre pronouncements given terrifying new credence by the cold, scientific language of Thorne's report. He was no longer just ranting; he was describing the *unidentified biological agent* in vivid, fearful terms.

"The report!" a voice boomed from the center of the hall. "Tell them about the report, Mayor!"

A young woman, a high school science teacher named Ms. Jenkins, stood up, clutching a printout of Thorne's paper. "Mayor Thompson, with all due respect, people need to understand what this report says. Dr. Thorne, a respected naturalist, has confirmed that the residue left by these incidents is unique. It doesn't match any known combustion. He explicitly states it points to an 'unidentified biological agent or atmospheric phenomenon'. That means it's not kids. It's not vandals. It's... something else. Something *living*." Her voice, though strained, carried authority.

The murmur turned into a roar. The fear in the hall coalesced into a desperate demand for action. People glanced around nervously, as if the very air might suddenly spark with fire.

Then, a new voice cut through the clamor. A voice as steady and unyielding as granite.

"We cannot stand idly by."

All eyes turned to the back of the hall. Silas Blackwood

stepped forward, his tall, lean frame cutting an imposing figure even in the crowded room. Blackwood was not a man given to grand gestures or emotional outbursts. A former big-game hunter who had retired to Oakhaven years ago, he was known for his stoic demeanor, his piercing gaze, and his reputation for ruthless efficiency. He rarely spoke at town meetings, preferring to observe, but when he did, everyone listened.

Blackwood moved through the crowd with an almost predatory grace, making his way to the front. He looked Chief Miller squarely in the eye, then turned to face the agitated citizens. His voice, though not loud, carried to every corner of the hall.

"Mayor Thompson, Chief Miller, my fellow Oakhavenites. We have been too passive. We have dismissed this as pranks, as imagination. But the evidence is now undeniable. Dr. Thorne's report, however clinical, confirms what some of us have long suspected." He paused, his gaze sweeping over the faces in the crowd, lingering for a moment on Fitzwilliam, who puffed out his chest in triumph.

"This is not a prankster. This is not a faulty wire. This is a creature. A creature that is stealing our cherished possessions, damaging our property, and now, threatening our sense of security." Blackwood's words were calm, logical, yet imbued with a chilling certainty. "We cannot wait for the police, stretched as they are, to solve a problem they are not equipped for. We cannot rely on luck. We must act."

A ripple of anticipation, a shift from fear to grim determination, went through the crowd. This was the kind of decisive leadership they craved.

"I propose," Blackwood continued, his voice gaining momentum, "the formation of a Neighborhood Watch and Creature Containment Unit." He held up a hand, forestalling any im-

CHAPTER 20

mediate questions. "This will be a volunteer force. We will organize patrols, share information, and establish a network of communication. We will utilize non-lethal methods – nets, tranquilizers, humane traps. Our goal is not to harm this... agent. Our goal is to contain it. To secure Oakhaven. To bring back our peace of mind."

He spoke of security, of order, of the safety of their families. He outlined a practical, organized approach, devoid of Fitzwilliam's sensationalism, yet acknowledging the underlying reality of the "creature." He emphasized community action, appealing to Oakhaven's inherent sense of self-reliance.

Gideon felt a cold dread wash over him. This was it. This was the hunt. Blackwood, with his calm authority and pragmatic language, was legitimizing the pursuit of Ingis.

"But Mr. Blackwood," Gideon interjected, his voice surprisingly weak amidst the rising murmurs of support, "have we considered all other possibilities? A unique atmospheric phenomenon, as Dr. Thorne suggested? Or perhaps a highly specialized... animal that's simply passing through?" He grasped at straws, desperate to plant a seed of doubt.

Blackwood turned his steely gaze on Gideon. "Mr. Croft, with all due respect to your admirable attempts to maintain journalistic objectivity, the evidence points to a creature that is neither atmospheric nor merely 'passing through.' It has established itself in Oakhaven. It has a pattern. And it is disrupting our lives. We must address this with the seriousness it deserves."

A chorus of agreement erupted from the crowd. "He's right!" "We need to act!" "Contain it!"

Gideon was shouted down, his questions lost in the rising tide of consensus. He looked at Chief Miller, hoping for some support, some logical counter-argument, but the Chief merely looked resigned, his face a portrait of weary acceptance. Even Ms. Jenkins, the science teacher, nodded, swayed by Blackwood's decisive pragmatism.

Mayor Thompson, seeing the overwhelming support, raised his hands. "All those in favor of forming the 'Neighborhood Watch and Creature Containment Unit,' please raise your hands."

A forest of hands shot up, almost unanimous. Gideon, isolated and powerless, kept his hands firmly in his lap. The motion passed overwhelmingly.

The meeting dissolved into a flurry of activity. Blackwood was immediately surrounded, eager volunteers stepping forward, offering their time, their tools, their determination. They spoke of patrol schedules, communication methods, and the need for vigilance. The fear hadn't vanished, but it had channeled itself into a grim, collective resolve.

Gideon slipped out of the crowded hall, the oppressive atmosphere replaced by the crisp night air. He walked quickly, his mind a whirlwind of despair. The hunt was on. Not a vague, unorganized search, but a coordinated, determined pursuit led by a man known for his efficiency and his ability to track. Ingis, his tiny, innocent dragon, was now the quarry.

He looked up at the moon, a pale sliver in the vast Oakhaven sky. Somewhere out there, Ingis was probably flitting between rooftops, oblivious to the net that was rapidly closing around it. Gideon felt a cold, crushing weight in his chest. He had to warn Ingis. He had to hide it. But how do you hide an impossible creature from an entire town that is now actively, legitimately, hunting for it? The midpoint of his extraordinary life had arrived, and it felt like the beginning of an inevitable, terrifying

CHAPTER 20

end.

Chapter 21

The crisp autumn air, once a symbol of Oakhaven's gentle transition, now felt charged, heavy with a grim new purpose. Silas Blackwood's words, delivered with chilling authority at the town hall meeting, had ignited a fire Gideon Croft feared he could never extinguish. The Neighborhood Watch and Creature Containment Unit was no longer a theoretical proposal; it was a tangible, organized force, its patrols beginning that very night. For Gideon, the town, once a mundane cage, had transformed into a sprawling, dangerous chessboard, and Ingis was the unwitting queen, hunted by zealous pawns.

The Unit wasted no time. Blackwood, true to his reputation for ruthless efficiency, had immediately set about organizing. Lists were drawn up, patrol routes assigned, and makeshift headquarters established in the dusty back room of the old hardware store. Volunteers, fueled by a potent cocktail of fear and civic duty, signed up in droves. They were armed not with weapons, but with flashlights, walkie-talkies, and a grim determination Gideon found terrifying.

Their initial strategy was simple, rudimentary, yet effective in Oakhaven's sleepy environment: surveillance and perimeter control. Patrols of two or three would walk specific routes, particularly around areas of previous "anomalies." Motion sensors, the kind used for security lights, were hastily rigged in alleyways and behind public buildings. Chief Miller, while still publicly maintaining a stance of caution, had subtly lent his support, advising on patrol techniques and even lending a few surplus police flashlights.

Gideon's days became a frantic, exhausting blur. His journalistic duties were now a thinly veiled cover for his true mission. He'd spend hours "interviewing" Unit volunteers, pretending to gather quotes for the *Gazette*, but in reality, meticulously noting their patrol schedules, their blind spots, their planned trap locations. He became a master of eavesdropping, lurking near Blackwood's makeshift HQ, straining to catch hushed conversations about "areas of interest" or "unusual activity."

His first encounter with a Unit trap was a chilling eye-opener. He was on one of his nightly patrols – ostensibly "gathering atmosphere" for a late-night feature – when he spotted it. Behind the library, nestled between two overgrown hedges, was a perfectly camouflaged net trap. It was a simple, humane design, weighted with sandbags, meant to spring upwards and ensnare anything that triggered the tripwire. A small, shiny piece of reflective tape had been placed at its center, a cruel, irresistible lure for Ingis.

Gideon's heart leaped into his throat. He looked around frantically. The alley was empty. He dropped to his knees, his fingers fumbling in the darkness. He carefully located the tripwire, then, with painstaking precision, disabled the tension mechanism, ensuring the net wouldn't spring. He then removed the shiny tape, replacing it with a dull, innocuous piece of plastic. He left the net in place, hoping it would simply remain dormant, an unseen monument to his intervention.

He found three more such nets that night, each near a location where Ingis had recently "acquired" an item. He disabled them all, his hands shaking with a mixture of fear and adrenaline. It was like playing a deadly, silent game of whack-a-mole.

Warning Ingis became Gideon's most pressing, and most challenging, task. How do you warn a tiny, instinct-driven dragon about human traps? He couldn't speak its language, and its understanding of abstract concepts like "danger" or "capture" was clearly limited. He resorted to a combination of visual cues and frantic, whispered pleas.

Whenever Ingis visited his apartment, Gideon would try to communicate the threat. He'd point to a diagram of a net he'd hastily sketched, then mimic a trapped animal, trying to convey panic. He'd then point to himself, then to Ingis, then shake his head violently, miming "no." Ingis would watch him with its bright, intelligent eyes, tilting its head, sometimes letting out a soft, confused chirrup. It seemed to understand his distress, if not the precise reason for it. Gideon sometimes thought he saw a flicker of apprehension in those fiery eyes, but it was impossible to be sure.

He also started leading Ingis away from known trap locations during their rare, brief encounters outside. If he saw Ingis flying towards an area he knew was booby-trapped, Gideon would quickly create a loud noise – a dropped camera, a shouted "Whoa!" – to startle Ingis and divert its flight path. He'd then try to lure it in a different direction with a piece of foil, a shiny button he carried for this very purpose.

Creating diversions became an essential part of Gideon's counter-insurgency. He couldn't just dismantle every trap; he needed to create new, misleading trails for the Unit. He started scattering small, shiny, but utterly worthless, objects in areas far from Ingis's actual known haunts – discarded bottle caps,

CHAPTER 21

broken pieces of mirror, even heavily polished stones. He'd "anonymously" tip off Chief Miller about these "new areas of interest," hoping to draw the Unit's patrols away from Ingis's real hunting grounds.

One night, he "discovered" a cluster of "suspicious" scorch marks on an old, disused barn on the far side of town, far from anything Ingis would be interested in. He even brought a small lighter and created a few rough, un-dragon-like burns to make the scene more convincing. The Unit descended on the barn the next day, wasting hours searching for non-existent evidence. Gideon watched from a distance, the guilt a familiar ache, but the necessity overriding it.

The emotional toll was immense. Sleep became a luxury he rarely afforded. He was constantly tired, his nerves frayed, his mind perpetually racing. Every creak of his apartment floorboards, every distant siren, sent a jolt of anxiety through him. He felt utterly alone in his secret, his only confidante a tiny dragon who understood trust, but not tactics.

His journalistic integrity, once his guiding star, was now a distant, flickering ember. He was lying constantly, manipulating information, and actively obstructing a town-wide effort. Brenda, his editor, noticed his increasing pallor and distracted air. "You're working too hard on these anomaly pieces, Gideon," she'd said, shaking her head. "Take a break. Get some sleep." She had no idea.

Silas Blackwood, the Unit's leader, was the most significant challenge. Blackwood was methodical, precise, and utterly relentless. He didn't scream or panic; he observed, he planned, he executed. Gideon saw him everywhere – leading patrols, reviewing maps, speaking in low, serious tones to his volunteers. Blackwood began to introduce more sophisticated elements: infrared motion sensors, then rudimentary 'trip-cameras' designed to capture images of anything moving past them.

Gideon had to adapt. Disabling the cameras became an intricate dance. He learned to approach from specific angles, using shadows and natural cover. He'd carry small, reflective pieces of aluminum foil, strategically placing them in front of the camera lenses to create lens flare, obscuring any actual image. He became an expert in the art of subterfuge, a ghost in Oakhaven's night.

One cold evening, Gideon was meticulously dismantling a pressure-plate trap near the old cannery when he heard voices. Two Unit members, their flashlights cutting through the darkness, were approaching his position. He froze, his heart hammering. He was caught.

He dove behind a stack of rusted barrels, barely fitting. He heard their footsteps, their hushed conversation. "Blackwood thinks it's heading this way," one whispered. "Saw some odd tracks near the old oak."

Gideon held his breath, pressing himself against the cold metal. He could hear them getting closer, their flashlights sweeping the area. He saw a beam of light fall directly on the trap he had just finished disabling. It looked untouched, an innocent patch of ground.

"Anything?" the second voice asked.

"Nah," the first replied, sighing. "Guess not. Let's check the perimeter by the old mill, like Blackwood said."

Their footsteps faded. Gideon remained hidden for several long minutes, trembling. He finally pushed himself out from behind the barrels, covered in dust and rust. It had been a near-miss, too close for comfort. His luck, he knew, wouldn't last

CHAPTER 21

forever.

As he walked home in the pre-dawn hours, the streets empty and silent, Gideon felt the profound loneliness of his impossible task. He was caught in a war he hadn't chosen, fighting an entire town to protect a creature that was oblivious to the stakes. He looked up at the clock tower, its golden key still missing, its silent face a constant reminder of the reason for the hunt. Somewhere, in its secret hoard, Ingis was likely sleeping, surrounded by its glittering treasures, unaware of the tightening net. And Gideon Croft, its sole guardian, was wide awake, ready to face another day of desperate counter-measures. The hunt was truly on, and Gideon was dangerously in the thick of it.

Chapter 22

The silent war Gideon Croft waged against the Neighborhood Watch and Creature Containment Unit escalated with each passing day. Silas Blackwood's methodical approach, devoid of the panic and sensationalism that fueled the average Oakhavenite, was proving to be a formidable threat. Gideon's frantic dismantling of traps and scattering of decoy shine could only go so far. He needed to be one step ahead, to anticipate the Unit's next move. And for that, he realized, he had to leverage the very access that defined his professional life: his journalistic credentials.

His role as a reporter for the *Oakhaven Gazette*, once a source of soul-crushing monotony, now became his most potent weapon. It provided him with an unimpeachable reason to be everywhere, to ask questions, to observe, to be granted access where an ordinary citizen would be met with suspicion. He transformed his daily routine into a sophisticated intelligence-gathering operation, his notepad and camera becoming tools of espionage rather than reporting.

The makeshift headquarters of the Unit, the dusty back room of the hardware store, became Gideon's primary target. He'd arrive ostensibly to "get a quote from Blackwood for the next edition," or to "profile the dedicated volunteers." Once inside,

CHAPTER 22

his eyes and ears were on high alert. He'd feign interest in a conversation with a volunteer about their "heroic efforts," subtly steering the discussion towards patrol schedules. "So, you're covering the north side tonight, eh? From the old mill to the creek?" he'd ask innocently, scribbling exaggerated notes about "civic pride." The volunteers, eager for positive media attention, would often provide details without realizing they were giving away critical tactical information.

He learned to read the wall maps that Blackwood had meticulously plastered with red and blue pins. Red pins, Gideon deduced, marked confirmed "anomaly" locations or areas of high surveillance. Blue pins indicated planned patrol routes or potential trap zones. While talking to a volunteer about the "best spots for a photo-op," he'd casually lean against the wall, absorbing the details of the map, committing patterns and proposed expansion zones to memory. His journalistic curiosity, so long a burden, was now his most powerful asset.

Blackwood himself was a tougher nut to crack. The former hunter was astute, his gaze piercing, and Gideon often felt the weight of Blackwood's suspicion, a silent challenge in the air between them. When Gideon attempted his usual subtle probing, Blackwood would offer only vague platitudes about "maintaining vigilance" and "following all leads." He never revealed specific plans.

So, Gideon shifted tactics. He started asking Blackwood seemingly innocuous questions about his hunting past, appealing to the man's ego and expertise. "Mr. Blackwood, given your extensive experience in tracking elusive game, what's your assessment of this... creature's intelligence?" he'd ask, leaning forward, feigning admiration. This would sometimes lead Blackwood into discussions about animal behavior, tracking techniques, and environmental patterns – all valuable insights for Gideon. He learned that Blackwood believed the "creature" was highly intelligent, capable of adapting, which only amplified Gideon's fear for Ingis.

He also found ways to "inadvertently" overhear conversations. He'd arrive early at the hardware store, before Blackwood or the core team, and "accidentally" leave his recorder running near a pile of boxes where he knew they held their strategy sessions. He'd come back later, retrieve it, and spend hours meticulously sifting through the muffled chatter, piecing together fragments of patrol changes, new trap designs, or planned stakeout points. The ethics of it were murky, at best, but Gideon had long since abandoned his journalistic purity in favor of Ingis's survival.

Once he had the intelligence, Gideon's next, equally critical, step was misinformation. He couldn't just dismantle traps; he had to actively steer the Unit away from Ingis's actual haunts. He became a ghost in Oakhaven's information network, subtly planting false leads that would consume the Unit's limited resources and precious time.

His primary method was through anonymous tips to other local reporters. He'd use burner phones, public Wi-Fi networks, and untraceable email accounts. He'd craft concise, intriguing messages that would pique a reporter's interest without revealing too much.

"Source indicates unusual activity, scorch marks near old mill. Suggest investigating during Tuesday night patrol." This would send the *Oakhaven Weekly* reporter scurrying to the mill, wasting their time, and crucially, drawing the Unit's patrols to a location Ingis rarely frequented.

He sometimes employed slightly more elaborate schemes.

CHAPTER 22

He'd "discover" a small, perfectly polished, but utterly worthless, piece of chrome embedded in the bark of a tree on the far side of the woods, miles from any of Ingis's known perching spots. He'd then "anonymously" call Chief Miller, hinting that "a concerned citizen noticed a strange metallic glint" and "a faint burnt smell" in that area. Miller, desperate for leads, would often dispatch a small team, including Blackwood, to investigate, effectively pulling them away from potential Ingis sightings.

Another tactic involved planting false "witness" accounts. He'd create anonymous social media profiles, or send letters to the *Gazette's* "Letters to the Editor" section under various pseudonyms. These accounts would describe sightings of "a large, shadowy bird" near the old cannery, or "a mischievous fox with glowing eyes" near the abandoned train tracks – areas where Ingis might briefly pass through, but certainly wouldn't establish a pattern. The vagueness was key; it allowed the Unit to invest time investigating, but offered no concrete evidence of a "biological agent."

He even used his own articles, subtly twisting the narrative. He'd write about the "Oakhaven Animal Control's diligent work in tracking down a particularly elusive coyote pack near the woods," subtly suggesting that the recent "animal" incidents were merely the work of mundane wildlife. He'd emphasize the difficulties of tracking any "wild animal" in Oakhaven's dense foliage, subtly preparing the public for the Unit's inevitable lack of concrete results.

The constant mental gymnastics were draining. Gideon felt like he was living two separate lives, the line between them blurring with each passing day. The guilt of his deception was a dull ache, but it was always overshadowed by the fierce, protective instinct he felt for Ingis. He'd watch the tiny dragon flitting playfully in his apartment, polishing a new acquisition with its tiny claws, and know that every lie, every misdirection, was worth it.

One particularly cold evening, Gideon was hunched over his laptop, sending out another anonymous tip about "unusual sounds" near the town's water tower. He heard a soft *clink* from his coffee table. Ingis had flown in, a gleaming silver button clutched in its talons. The button, Gideon recognized with a surge of dread, belonged to Mayor Thompson's ceremonial uniform, a replacement for the one Ingis had snatched at the press conference. Ingis nudged it towards Gideon, a silent offering of its newest, most significant treasure.

Gideon sighed, a mix of exasperation and profound affection. "Ingis," he whispered, "you're making this very, very hard."

He looked at the button, then back at his laptop screen, at the map of Oakhaven overlaid with Blackwood's projected patrol routes. The Unit was closing in, their methods growing more sophisticated. Gideon knew that his journalistic cunning, his mastery of information and misinformation, was Ingis's only defense. He had to keep digging, keep planting, keep lying. The fate of Oakhaven's most extraordinary secret, and perhaps even its tiny, innocent heart, rested solely on his ability to outwit the hunters, one anonymous tip, one false lead, at a time.

Chapter 23

The intelligence Gideon gathered, painstakingly sifting through overheard conversations and anonymous tips, painted an increasingly grim picture. Silas Blackwood's Unit was closing in, their methods evolving from rudimentary traps to more sophisticated, almost invisible snares. Gideon knew the locations of most of them, had even disabled a few, but he couldn't be everywhere at once. The constant stress gnawed at him, a persistent, low-grade fever that never quite broke.

One particularly blustery afternoon, the wind whipping through Oakhaven's streets, Gideon was theoretically "covering" a local school board meeting for the *Gazette*. In reality, he was glued to his laptop, scrutinizing a hastily scrawled map he'd found crumpled in the hardware store's waste bin. It was a partial schematic of a new, highly advanced net trap, marked "Phase 2 Deployment." The location: the old, disused botanical garden, a place Ingis frequently visited for its unique array of brightly colored, although not shiny, flowers.

His blood ran cold. The garden was a favorite napping spot for Ingis during the quieter hours, a place the dragon felt safe. Blackwood had clearly anticipated this. The notes indicated the net would be virtually undetectable, triggered by weight, designed to ensnare even the smallest of creatures.

He glanced at his watch. The school board meeting was dragging on, a monotonous drone about budget deficits. He couldn't leave without raising suspicion from Brenda, who was unusually attentive to his presence after the Mayor's button incident. But he couldn't wait. Every minute was crucial.

Just as he was contemplating a sudden, feigned illness, he heard a faint, familiar chirrup from outside the schoolhouse window. He peered through the blinds. Ingis. The tiny dragon was flitting amidst the autumn leaves of the ancient oak tree across the street, its emerald scales a vibrant contrast to the reds and golds. It seemed to be tracking something – a particularly iridescent beetle, perhaps. And its flight path was leading it directly towards the botanical garden.

Panic seized Gideon. He had to act. Now.

"Excuse me!" Gideon blurted out, startling the school board members. "Urgent... urgent news breaking! I have to go!" He grabbed his bag, ignoring Brenda's bewildered squawk of "Gideon! What?!"

He burst out of the schoolhouse, the blustery wind immediately pressing against him. He saw Ingis, still oblivious, heading straight for the garden's main gate. He ran, faster than he thought possible, his journalistic notebooks and pens rattling wildly in his bag.

He burst into the botanical garden, the air thick with the scent of damp earth and decaying leaves. He could see it: a barely visible shimmer of monofilament threads stretched taut across the main path, just beyond the ornate iron archway. The net was concealed beneath a layer of fallen leaves, perfectly hidden. And in the center, glinting innocently, was a discarded silver locket, a cruel, irresistible lure.

Ingis was perhaps fifty feet away, darting playfully, closing

CHAPTER 23

the distance rapidly. Gideon knew he couldn't disable the trap in time. He couldn't warn Ingis directly without exposing himself. He had only one option: create a diversion. A massive, undeniable, public diversion.

He looked around wildly. A stack of empty terracotta pots near a gardener's shed. A loose wheelbarrow.

Without thinking, Gideon changed direction, veering sharply towards the shed. He launched himself at the stack of pots, kicking them with all his might. The crash was deafening, a cascade of shattering clay and grinding ceramic. He then seized the wheelbarrow, its metal handles biting into his hands, and deliberately sent it careening into a row of decorative trellises. Wood splintered, metal shrieked, and a shower of colorful, dried flowers rained down.

The sudden, violent noise erupted through the quiet garden.

Ingis, startled by the cacophony, flinched mid-flight. The fiery sneeze erupted from its nostrils, a small, involuntary burst of light that momentarily illuminated the air around it. Its trajectory shifted, pulled off course by the unexpected sound. Instead of flying directly into the net, it veered sharply upwards, over the ornate archway, and zipped away, a blur of emerald and gold, into the safety of the nearby woods. It was gone.

Gideon breathed a shaky sigh of relief, his legs almost giving out. Ingis was safe.

But the silence that followed the crashing pots and splintering wood was deafening. And then, footsteps. Shouts.

"What in the blazes was that?!"

Chief Miller, alerted by the commotion, was already there, followed by two Unit volunteers, their faces etched with alarm. Blackwood, his expression grim and unwavering, was right behind them.

Gideon stood amidst the wreckage, breathing heavily, covered in dust and shards of terracotta. He looked like a madman, his hair disheveled, his eyes wide with a mixture of relief and fear.

"Croft! What in tarnation are you doing?!" Chief Miller demanded, his face a mixture of anger and utter disbelief. He gestured at the smashed pots, the splintered trellises.

Gideon struggled to form a coherent sentence. "I... I saw a... a very large crow! With a shiny object! It was trying to get into the garden! I just... I tried to scare it away!" He gestured vaguely at the sky, his hands still trembling.

Miller squinted at him, then at the wreckage. "A crow, Gideon? You just destroyed the town's botanical garden for a crow?" His voice was laced with suspicion.

Blackwood stepped forward, his gaze piercing. He didn't say a word, but his eyes swept over Gideon, then to the intact net, then back to Gideon. There was a calculating, knowing look in his eyes, a silent question that screamed: *You knew.*

The Unit volunteers, their initial alarm turning into confused glances, started whispering. "He's been acting strange." "Always at the scene of things." "That bee story was ridiculous."

Gideon felt their eyes on him, a hundred pairs of curious, suspicious gazes. He had saved Ingis, but at a tremendous cost. He had drawn a direct, undeniable spotlight onto himself. His frantic, desperate intervention had not only created a chaotic scene but had also put him squarely in a highly suspicious light. The illusionist had revealed his hand.

He looked from Miller's bewildered fury to Blackwood's chillingly analytical gaze. He was no longer just the reporter who saw things. He was now someone deeply, inexplicably involved. The near-miss hadn't been for Ingis; it had been for

Gideon himself. And this time, he hadn't managed to escape unseen.

Chapter 24

The destruction of the botanical garden, a frantic, public act of desperation, had irrevocably altered Gideon Croft's standing in Oakhaven. He was no longer just the town's cynical, slightly eccentric journalist; he was now the subject of bewildered whispers and outright suspicion. Chief Miller's patience was wearing thin, and Silas Blackwood's gaze, chillingly astute, seemed to follow Gideon wherever he went. The "crow with a shiny object" excuse had landed with a resounding thud, leaving Gideon exposed and vulnerable.

Among those who watched Gideon with particular interest was Dr. Aris Thorne. The naturalist had remained in Oakhaven, quietly continuing his scientific investigation, ostensibly collaborating with Chief Miller but largely operating independently. Thorne was a man of patterns, of data, of meticulous observation. He had read Gideon's initial articles, noting the precise details of the scorch marks, the peculiar nature of the missing items. He had even been intrigued by Gideon's bizarre theories about bioluminescent fungi and static squirrels. But the incident at the botanical garden, so dramatic and so out of character for a local reporter, had shifted his focus.

Thorne hadn't been at the school board meeting, but he had arrived at the botanical garden shortly after the commotion. He

CHAPTER 24

had observed Gideon, disheveled and frantic, amidst the shattered pots and splintered trellises. He had seen the bewildered expressions of Miller and Blackwood, and the silent, calculating look in Blackwood's eyes. And he had, with his scientific precision, noted the intact net trap, still hidden beneath the leaves, untouched by Gideon's apparent rampage.

This discrepancy sparked Thorne's keen intellect. Why would a reporter, ostensibly trying to catch a crow, cause such a dramatic, public spectacle? And why would he do it in a precise location where a highly sophisticated trap, designed for the "unidentified biological agent," was concealed?

From that day forward, Dr. Thorne's attention subtly but decisively shifted from merely analyzing scorch marks to observing Gideon Croft. He became Gideon's shadow, albeit a discreet one. Gideon, constantly on edge from Blackwood and Miller, rarely noticed Thorne's quiet presence. But Thorne was there, a silent, intellectual predator, piecing together a different kind of puzzle.

He began to notice Gideon's uncanny presence at every new incident. A valuable antique weathervane disappeared from the roof of the old gristmill, leaving its tell-tale scorch mark. Gideon was there, "reporting," but Thorne observed him subtly wiping at the residue, a small cloth hidden in his palm. When a gleaming brass bell vanished from the community center, Gideon was among the first on the scene, subtly nudging a dull coin into the bushes nearby as a false trail for the Unit.

Thorne noted Gideon's strange questions to Chief Miller – always pushing for simpler, more mundane explanations, even when the evidence defied them. He observed Gideon's body language, the way he subtly flinched at loud noises, the way his eyes would dart towards the sky when others were looking at the ground. He saw the peculiar intensity in Gideon's gaze whenever a new "anomaly" was reported, an intensity that spoke not of journalistic curiosity, but of personal investment.

He started cross-referencing Gideon's public actions with his private theories. Gideon's articles consistently downplayed the "creature" narrative, framing incidents as pranks or mundane animal activity, even as the scientific evidence (Thorne's own report!) pointed to something far more extraordinary. This contradiction, to Thorne's scientific mind, was highly significant. Why would a journalist, seemingly seeking the truth, actively suppress or misdirect from a truly groundbreaking phenomenon?

Thorne also noticed Gideon's strange interactions with Fitzwilliam. While Gideon publicly ridiculed the old man, Thorne observed him sometimes lingering near Fitzwilliam's rants, almost listening intently, a flicker of what Thorne interpreted as concern, not amusement, in his eyes. It was as if Gideon was gauging the impact of Fitzwilliam's words, not simply dismissing them.

He began to follow Gideon at a distance, particularly during the evening hours when Gideon would ostensibly be "gathering atmosphere" for his articles. He observed Gideon's strange detours, his careful approach to certain areas, the way he would sometimes kneel by a bush, or linger near a wall, almost as if he were tending to something unseen.

One blustery evening, Thorne was conducting a late-night survey of a recently scorched tree stump near the edge of the woods. He had set up a sensitive audio recorder, hoping to capture any unusual sounds. As he was packing up, he saw Gideon Croft, several hundred yards away, moving stealthily through the undergrowth. Gideon was talking, his voice a low,

CHAPTER 24

soothing murmur, seemingly to himself. Then, Thorne saw it: a tiny, almost imperceptible flash of emerald green, briefly visible as it darted from a low branch, heading towards Gideon, before vanishing.

Thorne froze, his breath catching. He hadn't seen it clearly, but the flash, combined with Gideon's strange behavior, sent a jolt of recognition through him. This was beyond coincidence. This was beyond any conventional explanation.

He returned to his temporary lodging in Oakhaven, his mind alight. He pulled out his own notebooks, filled with meticulous data on scorch marks, chemical residues, and now, observations of Gideon Croft. He laid them all out. The missing objects. The unique scorch marks. Fitzwilliam's bizarrely accurate ramblings. His own scientific findings. And Gideon Croft, the anomaly within the anomaly, always present, always deflecting, always acting strangely.

Thorne sat back, a slow, contemplative smile spreading across his face. He didn't know *what* Gideon was protecting. He didn't know *how* Gideon was connected. But he knew, with a certainty that thrilled his scientific soul, that Gideon Croft was not just a reporter covering a story. He was a guardian. And Thorne, now, would watch Gideon Croft even more closely than he watched the scorch marks themselves. The truth, whatever it was, was hidden with Gideon, and Thorne was determined to uncover it.

Chapter 25

The chill in the Oakhaven air deepened with the onset of late autumn, mirroring the escalating tension that now gripped the town. Dr. Aris Thorne's quiet, focused observations had added another layer of invisible pressure on Gideon Croft, but the immediate, visceral threat still emanated from Silas Blackwood and his increasingly determined Neighborhood Watch and Creature Containment Unit. The initial, rudimentary efforts had yielded no results, and Blackwood, a man unaccustomed to failure, was growing visibly frustrated. His quiet determination, once a reassuring presence for the town, now had a razor's edge.

The lack of success had a polarizing effect on Oakhaven. Some citizens, weary of the constant vigilance and the persistent unease, began to whisper doubts. Perhaps Fitzwilliam was just crazy after all. Perhaps the "creature" was a collective delusion. But for a larger, more vocal segment, the frustration only intensified their fear and their resolve. The absence of a tangible capture fueled their anxieties, turning their fear into a simmering anger that sought an outlet. Blackwood, sensing this shift, capitalized on it, channeling their apprehension into renewed, more aggressive action.

The first sign of the escalation came with a town-wide announcement, disseminated through flyers and the *Gazette* (where Gideon had no choice but to print it, feeling a familiar pang of complicity). It called for increased public participation, for residents to report "any unusual glimmer, sound, or unusual aerial activity, however fleeting." It also outlined new, more sophisticated methods the Unit would be deploying.

Blackwood's next move was the introduction of sonic disruptors. These were small, discreet devices, usually hidden in bushes or on lampposts near known "anomaly" hotspots. They emitted a high-frequency sound, inaudible to most humans, but designed to be irritating or disorienting to small animals. The idea was to flush out the "creature" from its hiding places, forcing it into the open. Gideon, reading the technical specifications he'd managed to pilfer from Blackwood's notes, knew the sonic frequency was precisely within the range that might affect a creature with heightened senses, like Ingis.

His frantic attempts to counter these became a dangerous game of hide-and-seek. He'd locate the devices using his own sensitive audio equipment (a directional microphone he'd originally bought for discreet interviews) and disable them, often under the cover of darkness. This required navigating dark alleyways, climbing fences, and crawling through dense foliage, all while avoiding Unit patrols. One night, he almost triggered a motion-activated spotlight attached to a sonic disruptor, narrowly escaping detection by diving into a thorny rose bush. He emerged scratched and bleeding, but the device was silenced.

Next came the thermal imaging cameras. These were deployed on rooftops, atop the town hall, and even secretly integrated into the town's new (and previously benign) public security camera network. These cameras, Blackwood explained to the Unit, could detect even the smallest heat signature, making it impossible for the "creature" to move unseen, especially during the cold autumn nights. For Ingis, a tiny creature whose fiery sneezes meant it emanated heat, these cameras were a death sentence for its secrecy.

Gideon's counter-measures for the thermal cameras were even more desperate. He couldn't disable them all. He resorted to covering lenses with mud or dense foliage where possible, but this was too obvious. He began experimenting with reflective blankets and aluminum foil, trying to create "cold spots" or false heat signatures that would obscure Ingis's actual presence. He spent hours in his apartment, Ingis chirping curiously as he draped foil over household objects, trying to understand how to mask a heat signature. He even attempted to create "decoy" heat sources – small, battery-operated hand warmers attached to kites or drones he'd fly discreetly in other parts of town, hoping to draw the Unit's attention away. The problem was, Ingis was mobile, and Gideon couldn't possibly provide continuous cover.

Blackwood also introduced pheromone traps. These were less about capturing and more about luring. Based on a theoretical analysis of what might attract an "unidentified biological agent," they contained various strong, sweet, or metallic scents, designed to draw the creature into open areas where the Unit could then observe or attempt containment. The golden key's scent, for example, had been meticulously recreated in a few of these traps. Gideon, observing Ingis's uncanny attraction to meaningful items, knew these would be a significant lure. He'd try to neutralize the pheromones with strong, neutralizers he'd bought from a hunting supply store, or simply move the traps to less populated areas.

The most elaborate, and terrifying, traps were the multilayered containment nets. These were larger than the previous ones, often covering entire sections of abandoned buildings or large, overgrown patches of land. They were designed with multiple tripwires, infrared sensors, and even pressure plates, all linked to trigger spring-loaded nets that would rise rapidly, creating a sealed enclosure. Blackwood's detailed plans for these, meticulously drawn, showed a chilling understanding of how to corner an elusive, fast-moving target. Gideon had to use every ounce of his stealth and cunning to find these, often crawling through tight spaces and navigating treacherous terrain, just to snip a single wire.

The town itself became a landscape of paranoia. Neighbors watched neighbors. Every shadow seemed to harbor a secret. Children whispered stories of the "Oakhaven Ghost Fire." Fitzwilliam's rants, now less outlandish and more prophetic, were listened to with grim, wide-eyed attention. The once-charming "Pumpkin Patch Parade" had been canceled, deemed too risky. The sense of community spirit was replaced by a collective fear that manifested in vigilance and suspicion.

Gideon felt the weight of it all pressing down on him. His exhaustion was bone-deep, his nerves frayed to a fine thread. He barely slept, waking at every creak of his apartment, every distant siren. He was constantly running, constantly planning, constantly deceiving. Brenda, his editor, tried to intervene. "Gideon, you look terrible. You're obsessed with these stories. Take a break." But Gideon knew he couldn't.

One late night, while attempting to disable a thermal camera mounted on the roof of the old post office, Gideon heard the distinct crackle of a walkie-talkie nearby. He froze, pressed against the cold, grimy brickwork.

"Blackwood to Unit 3. Heat signature detected near the

old library. Moving fast. Proceed with caution. Repeat, heat signature detected."

Gideon's heart seized. The old library. Ingis's favorite napping spot during the day, relatively safe. But at night, with thermal cameras... He had to get there.

He scrambled off the roof, ignoring the scraped skin and bruised knees. He ran through the dark streets, trying to reach the library before Blackwood's Unit. As he neared, he saw the faint, tell-tale red glow of infrared lights emanating from the building. Two Unit members, their faces grim, were already moving in, their flashlights cutting through the darkness.

Gideon saw a tiny, emerald flash dart from a window, barely visible even to his practiced eyes. Ingis. It had been inside. It had escaped. But the Unit was closer than ever.

He heard Blackwood's voice, calm and precise, giving orders into his walkie-talkie. "It's moving towards the park. Unit 1, head for the treeline. Unit 2, sweep the playground. Containment Protocol Alpha initiated."

Gideon watched Ingis disappear into the night, a tiny, vulnerable spark against the vast, dark sky. He had bought it time, just barely. But the escalation was undeniable. Blackwood was methodical, relentless. The hunt was no longer just a local effort; it was a sophisticated, technologically-driven pursuit. And Gideon knew, with a chilling certainty, that the next "near miss" might very well be a capture. The noose was tightening, and Gideon, exhausted and isolated, felt the desperate urgency of a man running out of options. The fate of Ingis, and the very soul of Oakhaven, hung precariously in the balance.

Chapter 26

Gideon Croft ran, the cold Oakhaven night wind tearing at his clothes, the crackle of Blackwood's walkie-talkie echoing in his ears: "Heat signature detected near the old library... Containment Protocol Alpha initiated." His lungs burned, his legs ached, but the image of Ingis, tiny and vulnerable, trapped within the methodical grip of the Unit, propelled him forward. He had seen the emerald flash from the library window, seen Ingis dart into the night, but what had it left behind? What evidence of its frantic escape?

He burst into the square where the old Oakhaven Library stood, its gothic architecture silhouetted against the meager moonlight. The Unit was already converging. Flashlights cut through the darkness like probing eyes. Two Unit members, their faces grim, were just entering the main doors, while Chief Miller's patrol car pulled up, lights flashing, followed closely by Silas Blackwood's imposing figure.

Gideon slid to a halt behind a thick oak tree, catching his breath. He saw the faint, tell-tale glow of thermal cameras on the roof of the adjacent building, sweeping the library's exterior. He had to get inside. He had to assess the damage, the evidence, before Blackwood's keen eyes and the Unit's systematic search uncovered anything irrefutable.

Feigning his journalistic role, Gideon approached Chief Miller, out of breath. "Chief! What's happened? I heard a commotion!"

Miller, looking harried, gestured vaguely towards the library. "Heat signature. Blackwood's got one of his fancy cameras. Something was in there. It got out, but we need to sweep the area. Make sure it didn't leave anything behind."

"I'll go in with them," Gideon offered quickly, his voice tight. "Get the story. Document the search."

Miller, grateful for the extra pair of eyes and the potential for positive media coverage, nodded. "Alright, Croft. But stick with the Unit. Don't touch anything."

Gideon muttered an assent and slipped past, his heart pounding. He entered the library, the grand, cavernous space now transformed into a tense, silent hunting ground. The Unit members moved with a practiced precision Gideon found terrifying. They fanned out, flashlights sweeping over dusty bookshelves, whispering into their walkie-talkies.

Gideon moved deeper into the stacks, his eyes frantically searching. He needed to find whatever Ingis had left behind. He remembered Ingis's love for hiding in secluded, often overlooked spots. His gaze fell upon the section dedicated to Oakhaven's local history – a dark, quiet alcove tucked away from the main reading room. Ingis had often been spotted there, drawn to the old, leather-bound chronicles and the tarnished silver bookmarks.

As he approached the alcove, a wave of apprehension washed over him. The air here felt different, a faint, acrid scent of ozone mingling with the musty smell of old paper. And then he saw it.

On the floor, nestled between a forgotten armchair and a towering shelf of ancient tomes, was a patch of darkened, singed carpet. It was larger than any scorch mark he'd seen

Ingis create before, almost the size of a dinner plate, and the fibers were still faintly smoldering, a thin wisp of smoke curling upwards. It was clear that Ingis, startled by the thermal camera detection and the Unit's rapid approach, had unleashed a panicked, powerful sneeze. This wasn't a playful puff; this was a desperate burst of defensive fire.

But it wasn't just the carpet. Directly above the scorched area, hanging precariously from a high window, was a section of the library's heavy, velvet curtains. The bottom edge, where it had likely brushed against Ingis during its frantic escape, was blackened and frayed, still glowing with a faint, angry ember. This was the "curtains ablaze" moment, literal and terrifying. The damage was undeniable, a clear, unmistakable sign of Ingis's presence, and its desperate escape.

Gideon froze, his mind racing. This was too big to explain away as a misplaced cigarette or a faulty lamp. The Unit would find it. Blackwood would find it. And then Ingis's secret would be out.

He heard footsteps approaching, the distinct crunch of Chief Miller's heavy boots. Gideon knew he had seconds. He had to cover it up. But how? He couldn't put out a smoldering carpet without drawing immediate attention. He couldn't hide the scorched curtains.

His eyes darted around the alcove, desperate. He saw an old, heavy wooden fire extinguisher cabinet mounted on the wall, long forgotten and probably empty. Above it, a small, decorative tapestry, depicting a faded Oakhaven landscape, hung askew.

A frantic, desperate idea sparked in his mind.

As Miller's footsteps grew closer, Gideon acted. He grabbed the heavy armchair, grunting with effort, and swiftly dragged it over the scorched carpet, completely obscuring the worst of the burn. He then reached up, his fingers fumbling, and pulled the old tapestry off its hooks. With a rapid, jerky movement, he swung the tapestry over the damaged curtains, covering the singed velvet completely. It hung unevenly, but from a quick glance, it looked like old, undisturbed decor.

He heard Miller's voice. "Anything, Unit 4?"

"Negative, Chief. Perimeter clear. No signs of... anything."

Gideon quickly moved to a nearby shelf, pretending to be examining a book, his back to the covered evidence. He could hear Miller and Blackwood entering the section.

"Nothing here, Chief," a Unit member said, his flashlight sweeping the shelves.

"Check the corners," Blackwood's voice was calm, methodical. "Heat signatures often lead to sheltered areas."

Gideon held his breath. He heard them approach the alcove. He could feel their presence, their flashlights dancing on the shelves. He prayed his frantic cover-up would hold.

"Hmm," Blackwood murmured, his voice closer now. "This armchair seems... recently moved."

Gideon's heart leaped. He braced himself.

"Perhaps the librarian was cleaning," Chief Miller offered, his voice sounding tired. "It's an old library, Blackwood. Things shift."

Gideon risked a quick glance over his shoulder. Blackwood was standing right beside the armchair, his gaze fixed on the tapestry covering the curtains. His eyes were narrowed, perceptive. He looked like he was seconds away from pulling the armchair aside, from sweeping the tapestry away.

"The air here," Blackwood noted, taking a slow sniff. "A faint... acrid scent. Like burnt sugar."

CHAPTER 26

Miller sighed. "Old wiring, Blackwood. This place is ancient. Probably some dust burning off a faulty bulb."

Blackwood didn't respond directly. He simply stared at the armchair, then at the tapestry. Gideon felt a bead of sweat trickle down his spine. It was a terrifying stalemate, a silent battle of wills.

Then, to Gideon's immense relief, Blackwood merely grunted. "Perhaps. Let's move on. I want a full sweep of the basement and the old archives."

The footsteps receded. Gideon remained frozen, his back to the alcove, until the last whisper of their voices faded. He slowly exhaled, his lungs burning. He had done it. He had bought Ingis time. He had covered its tracks.

But the close call had been too close. The sheer size of the scorch mark, the damaged curtain – Ingis was getting bolder, its reactions more dramatic, and its presence harder to conceal. He couldn't keep doing this indefinitely. He needed a permanent solution. He needed to find Ingis's hoard.

He walked back to the alcove, pulling the armchair away, revealing the singed carpet. He looked up at the damaged curtains, now half-hidden by the tapestry. His eyes scanned the wall behind the shelves, searching for anything. He needed to find Ingis's hiding place, the one central location where all the shiny treasures were stored. That golden key *had* to be there.

He ran his hand along the dusty spine of an old, heavy tome on a bottom shelf. His fingers brushed against something. A faint click. He pressed harder. The book shifted inwards.

Gideon's breath hitched. He pushed the book further, and with a soft groan, a section of the bookshelf, perhaps three feet wide, swung inward, revealing a dark, narrow passage. The air from within was still, undisturbed, carrying a faint, undeniable scent of ozone and something else – a delicate, metallic shimmer.

He peered into the darkness, pulling out his phone and turning on the flashlight. The beam cut through the gloom, revealing a cramped, dusty tunnel. And at the end of the tunnel, a faint, almost magical glimmer.

It wasn't just a glimmer. It was a thousand glimmers. The light bounced off countless surfaces: coins, thimbles, lockets, keys, watches, and a myriad of other precious, shiny objects. All meticulously arranged, creating a dazzling, impossible tapestry of light. And at the very center, catching the light more brilliantly than anything else, was the gleaming, ornate golden key to the clock tower.

Gideon felt a profound, almost dizzying sense of awe. This was it. This was Ingis's secret sanctuary. The hoard. The solution to everything. He looked back at the main library, at the faint sounds of the Unit's methodical search. He had to be quick. He had to get inside.

He took a deep breath, the stale air of the passage filling his lungs. He was Gideon Croft, journalist. And now, he was standing at the threshold of the greatest discovery of his life, a secret passage leading to a dragon's treasure hoard. The "curtains ablaze" near-disaster had, against all odds, led him directly to Ingis's hidden world. He pushed the bookshelf open wider and stepped into the darkness, into the impossible.

Chapter 27

The shimmering cascade of Oakhaven's lost treasures, bathed in the beam of Gideon's phone light, was breathtaking. Thimbles, lockets, watches, keys – a glittering tapestry of stolen significance. And at its heart, the golden clock tower key, radiating a brilliant luster. Gideon stood at the entrance of Ingis's secret hoard, a profound sense of awe warring with a fresh, overwhelming wave of despair. He had found the problem, but solving it felt more impossible than ever. The narrow, dusty tunnel, breathing the musty scent of ancient paper and the faint, sweet metallic tang of Ingis's presence, felt less like a discovery and more like the opening of Pandora's box.

The hoard was a beautiful, chaotic testament to Ingis's primal instincts, but it was also a ticking time bomb. Every single piece was evidence. Every glint of gold and silver was a direct link to the "anomalies" that had gripped Oakhaven, each one carefully cataloged in his mental anomaly log. Retrieving the clock tower key was suddenly not enough. This wasn't about returning a single item; it was about halting an instinct older than Oakhaven itself. He needed to get Ingis to stop collecting. He needed to make it *understand* the danger, the human concept of consequence and capture.

He carefully stepped into the cramped, dust-filled tunnel, his flashlight illuminating the dazzling collection. Ingis was nowhere in sight. It had likely darted away after its panicked sneeze in the library, seeking refuge elsewhere, its simple mind already moved past the stressful encounter. Gideon spent a few moments, trying to commit the layout of the hoard to memory, noting the unique items, the sheer volume, the almost artistic arrangement of the glittering trove. It was far more extensive than he had ever imagined, a dizzying testament to Ingis's tireless efforts and Oakhaven's overlooked wealth.

Later that night, back in the relative safety of his apartment, the weight of the hoard, and the task it represented, settled heavily upon Gideon. He found Ingis perched on his bookshelf, meticulously polishing a newly acquired, gleaming silver earring. It chirped contentedly, seemingly oblivious to the recent near-capture or the discovery of its secret lair, its tiny claws delicately buffing the metal to a brilliant sheen.

Gideon gently scooped Ingis up, holding it carefully in his cupped hands, feeling the light, warm flutter of its small body. "Ingis," he began, his voice strained with an urgency that bordered on desperation, "we need to talk. This isn't a game anymore. You can't keep doing this." He brought his phone closer, displaying a news article he'd drafted about the increased Unit patrols, a blurry photo of Blackwood's grim, determined face plastered next to a headline about "Community Vigilance." "They're hunting you. They're setting traps. They almost had you tonight, at the library. You caused that big burn trying to get away."

Ingis tilted its head, its fiery eyes blinking, reflecting the phone screen's light. It then playfully nipped at Gideon's finger, a gentle, almost affectionate gesture, letting out a soft, bell-like chuckle that resonated deep within Gideon's palm. It seemed to view Gideon's frantic gestures and distressed tone as part of a new, curious game, a lively interaction rather than a grave warning. Its tiny antennae-like feelers twitched, sensing Gideon's emotions, but translating them into something akin to excited human chatter.

Gideon sighed, rubbing his temples with his free hand. How do you explain the concept of human laws, of ownership, of danger and confinement, to a creature driven by an ancient, instinctual desire for glitter? Ingis didn't understand property rights. It didn't comprehend consequences beyond the immediate thrill of acquisition. To it, shiny objects existed to be admired, collected, cherished. They were simply beautiful, glowing things that called to its very essence. And the thrill of acquiring a *new* shiny object, especially one that vibrated with human significance – a treasured heirloom, a symbol of civic pride – was an irresistible, almost spiritual pull. Its hoard wasn't about possession in the human sense; it was about the continuous hunt, the joy of the gleam, the accumulating beauty.

He tried a different approach, a futile attempt at negotiation. He took out a handful of polished pennies, the kind he used to divert Ingis when he couldn't replace a stolen item without drawing attention. He offered them, splaying them out on his palm. "Look, Ingis. These are shiny. Just as shiny. You have all these, you don't need more. Stay here. Stay safe."

Ingis gave the pennies a cursory sniff, its tiny nostrils flaring, then turned its head, its gaze drifting towards Gideon's own watch, its polished metal glinting faintly in the lamplight. A tiny puff of smoke escaped its nostrils, a clear sign of renewed, preferential interest. The pennies, however shiny, lacked the *meaningful* allure, the human story, the subtle vibrational hum of a cherished heirloom or a significant civic artifact. They were mere baubles, easily dismissed.

Gideon felt the overwhelming weight of his impossible task. He was trying to control an animalistic instinct, to reason with a creature whose very existence defied logic and scientific understanding. He couldn't possibly keep Ingis contained in his small apartment forever; it was a wild, free creature, meant to soar and explore. And even if he could, its deep-seated, instinctual desire for new, significant shiny objects would inevitably drive it out, a force of nature as unyielding as the tides.

The loneliness of his secret pressed down on him, heavier than ever before. He was the only one who knew, the only one who truly understood Ingis's innocence and its danger. He couldn't tell Chief Miller, who would dismiss his story as a delusion and immediately try to capture the dragon, likely using methods that would harm it. He couldn't tell Brenda, who would think he'd finally cracked under the pressure of small-town journalism, perhaps recommending a long vacation or even early retirement. And he certainly couldn't tell Dr. Thorne, who, despite his scientific curiosity, would approach Ingis with a desire to study, to categorize, to contain, ultimately leading to a life in a laboratory.

He thought of the Unit patrols, now more frequent, more systematic, their nets and sensors spreading like a slow, deliberate disease across Oakhaven. He imagined Blackwood's grim, unyielding determination, his relentless tracking methods, the meticulous planning Gideon had secretly observed. He knew Thorne was watching him, piecing together his strange behavior, observing his erratic responses to the "anomalies." Gideon was caught between an increasingly sophisticated, technologically advanced hunt and a completely oblivious, utterly charming, and inherently uncontrollable dragon. It was a suffocating pressure from all sides, and he was the solitary fulcrum point.

He tried creating "safe zones" outside his apartment, meticulously clearing small, hidden nooks in the old, disused botanical garden or in abandoned construction sites. He'd scatter new, tempting, but ultimately worthless, shiny objects within these cleared spaces – carefully chosen reflective surfaces, scraps of gleaming aluminum, polished glass. He hoped Ingis would be satisfied with these offerings, that its desire for novelty and glitter could be satiated without risk to itself or Oakhaven's treasured possessions. He'd watch from a distance, binoculars trained, praying Ingis would choose the safe gleam over the dangerous allure of a golden pocket watch or a gleaming brooch on someone's lapel. Sometimes it worked. Often, it didn't. He'd arrive at a scene of a new "theft" to find the fake shine untouched, and the real item gone, leaving behind its faint scorch mark, a testament to his repeated failures.

The constant tension, the relentless vigilance, began to take its toll. Gideon found himself utterly exhausted, perpetually wired on caffeine and adrenaline. He barely slept, waking at every unfamiliar sound, every rustle of leaves outside his window. His meals were often forgotten, his apartment a controlled chaos of maps, notes, and various shiny trinkets, both real and decoy. He was losing weight, his face gaunt, his eyes perpetually shadowed, reflecting the sleepless nights and the weight of his impossible burden. The lines of cynicism that had once defined his face were now etched deeper, but they were lines born of weary responsibility, not detached amusement.

Yet, despite the exhaustion, despite the seemingly impossible nature of his task, Gideon's affection for Ingis only deepened. When Ingis would land softly on his shoulder, its tiny claws a feather-light touch, and let out a soft, contented purr, a warmth would spread through him, piercing the veil of his profound loneliness. It was a unique, profound bond, forged in secret and sustained by mutual trust. He was Ingis's only chance for survival in a world that would inevitably crush it, and that crushing responsibility, however immense, was also his purpose, the very core of his new, precarious existence.

He knew he couldn't force Ingis to change its nature. He couldn't stop it from being a dragon, driven by its primal instincts. The struggle wasn't about controlling Ingis; it was about managing the inevitable collision between Ingis's ancient, instinctual world and Oakhaven's orderly, possessive human society. He was a translator, a mediator, a desperate shield. And the weight of that truth, the sheer, crushing impossibility of it all, settled heavily on Gideon Croft's shoulders, leaving him alone with his secret, and his beloved, mischievous, and utterly uncontrollable dragon. The hoard, glittering in the secret passage of the library, waited, a symbol of both Ingis's unyielding nature and the impossible depth of Gideon's commitment.

Chapter 28

The crispness of the late autumn air in Oakhaven had settled into a biting cold, mirroring the frost that had begun to coat Gideon Croft's nerves. The secret of Ingis, once a thrilling revelation, was now a constant, agonizing pressure. The relentless vigilance, the ceaseless attempts to misdirect Dr. Thorne, to sabotage Blackwood's Unit, and to negotiate with a dragon's primordial instincts, had stripped Gideon bare, leaving him perpetually exhausted and isolated. He was a tightly wound spring, waiting for the inevitable snap.

The town square, usually a sleepy tableau of park benches and the gurgling fountain, had become the psychological heart of Oakhaven's growing paranoia. It was here that Mayor Thompson had made his ill-fated press conference, here that Fitzwilliam continued his prophetic rants, and it was here that Blackwood's Unit often converged, their methodical patrols a constant, unsettling presence. For Gideon, the square felt less like a public space and more like a stage set for a tragedy he was desperate to prevent.

Blackwood, with his hunter's patience and tactical mind, had escalated his efforts. His latest strategy was a series of meticulously placed "observation points" around the square, camouflaged and equipped with upgraded thermal imaging, high-resolution cameras, and sensitive audio recorders. These weren't traps in the physical sense, but an invisible net designed to pinpoint the "creature's" movements, to build a definitive behavioral profile before a final, decisive containment. He'd even subtly introduced a new lure: a small, intricately carved silver bird, designed to catch the faintest light, placed conspicuously on the lip of the fountain. It hummed with a quiet, alluring gleam, an irresistible temptation for Ingis.

Gideon had discovered the observation points only by sheer luck, noticing an unusual glint high on the clock tower's face, too small to be anything but a lens. He spent a frantic evening trying to disable what he could, but Blackwood was too good. There were too many, too well-hidden. He knew it was only a matter of time before Ingis walked, or rather, flew, into view.

That fateful Tuesday afternoon began like any other, deceptively calm. Gideon was "reporting" on a relatively quiet municipal building committee meeting – a dull affair that allowed him to keep one eye on his phone, which showed a live, though grainy, feed from a compromised public camera near the square. He'd hacked into Oakhaven's nascent security system weeks ago, another blurry line crossed in his personal ethics.

Suddenly, a tiny, emerald green flicker appeared on his screen. Ingis. It was perched on the old oak tree, its head cocked, its fiery eyes fixed on the gleaming silver bird on the fountain. It was mesmerized.

Gideon's heart lurched. "No, Ingis," he muttered under his breath, his voice barely audible above the droning committee debate. "Don't."

He watched, helpless, as Ingis launched itself from the tree. It was a fluid, graceful arc, a tiny, living jewel cutting through the autumn air, straight for the fountain. Blackwood's gamble had paid off.

"I need to go," Gideon mumbled, pushing back his chair, startling Brenda, who was mid-sentence about budgetary allocations. "Emergency! Major news break!"

He didn't wait for an answer, sprinting out of the building. The town square was bustling, a scattering of late-afternoon strollers, parents with children, and the usual gaggle of gossiping retirees. Chief Miller's patrol car was parked idly near the diner. Blackwood himself, Gideon knew from his intel, was likely in the concealed observation post in the clock tower's belfry, a perfect vantage point.

Gideon burst into the square, his eyes immediately locking onto the fountain. Ingis was there, perched on the edge, its tiny claws delicately touching the silver bird. It chirped with delight, a soft, bell-like sound that was lost in the general hum of the square. A plume of smoke, a tiny expression of joy, curled from its nostrils.

Then, the sudden, sharp crackle of Chief Miller's walkie-talkie. "Heat signature confirmed! Visual confirmation! Target acquired at fountain!" Miller's voice, usually calm, was laced with an undeniable tension.

"Unit 1, initiate perimeter lockdown! Unit 2, prepare containment nets!" Blackwood's voice, cold and precise, barked over the radio, loud enough for Gideon to hear.

Gideon looked around. Blackwood's Unit, seemingly from nowhere, began to converge. Two men emerged from the shadows of the old bank building, carrying what looked like collapsible nets. Another pair started cordoning off the square, gently but firmly ushering surprised citizens away. Chief Miller was already moving, his hand on his sidearm, not drawing it, but ready.

Ingis, startled by the sudden human commotion, looked up. Its fiery eyes widened. It chirped frantically, a sound of alarm, a tiny puff of smoke escaping its nostrils. It snatched the silver bird, its instinct to collect overriding its instinct to flee.

Gideon knew this was it. Ingis was cornered. There was nowhere for it to go. Blackwood had anticipated every escape route. The observation cameras were surely capturing every detail. Gideon had seconds, maybe less, before Ingis was ensnared, its secret brutally exposed, its freedom irrevocably lost.

He scanned the square, his mind racing, desperate. He needed a distraction. A big one. Something that would throw the entire operation into chaos. His eyes landed on the town's old, notoriously temperamental fire alarm, mounted prominently on the side of the municipal building. It was an antiquated lever system, prone to false alarms, but it was loud. Very loud. And directly across the square.

Without hesitation, Gideon sprinted. He pushed past startled pedestrians, ignored the shouts from Chief Miller. His eyes were fixed on the fire alarm, his legs pumping with a frantic, desperate energy.

"Hey! What are you doing?!" a Unit member shouted, seeing Gideon's sudden, inexplicable dash.

Gideon reached the alarm box, his fingers fumbling for the lever. He ripped open the glass cover, ignoring the sharp pain as glass shards bit into his palm. He pulled the lever down with all his might.

The wail was deafening. A piercing, ear-splitting shriek that tore through the quiet afternoon, echoing off the surrounding buildings. It was chaotic, terrifying. Citizens screamed, chil-

CHAPTER 28

dren cried, covering their ears. The Unit members, caught off guard, stumbled, their concentration shattered. Chief Miller swore loudly, his hand flying to his ear to adjust his ringing walkie-talkie.

"False alarm! False alarm!" he yelled into the static. "Everyone, calm down! It's a false alarm!"

But the siren was too loud, too persistent. Panic erupted. People began to run, stampeding in confused directions, creating a swirling vortex of human chaos. The containment nets, half-deployed, became tangled in the panicked crowd. The Unit members struggled to maintain order, their focus diverted from the fountain.

In the midst of the pandemonium, Gideon saw it. Ingis. Startled by the deafening siren, it had let out a desperate, fiery sneeze – a visible burst of flame that illuminated its terrified eyes – and then, seizing the moment of utter human disarray, it launched itself into the sky. It darted upwards, a tiny, emerald streak vanishing into the gathering clouds, carrying the silver bird with it. It was gone. Free.

Gideon stood by the wailing fire alarm, his hand still on the lever, his chest heaving. The siren continued its ear-splitting shriek. The square was a scene of utter pandemonium. Chief Miller was yelling into his walkie-talkie, his face a mask of furious exasperation. Blackwood, emerging from the clock tower, his face dark with frustrated rage, fixed his gaze on Gideon.

"CROFT!" Chief Miller bellowed, his voice hoarse, finally tearing himself away from the chaos. He stormed towards Gideon, his face purple with fury. "What in the blazes did you just do?!"

Gideon released the lever, the siren dying with a drawn-out, agonizing wail, leaving a ringing silence in its wake. He felt a fresh sting from the cuts on his hand. He looked at Miller, then at Blackwood, whose cold, calculating eyes were now entirely fixed on him.

"I... I thought I saw smoke, Chief," Gideon stammered, his voice weak. "Coming from the municipal building. I thought it was a real fire." It was a pathetic, transparent lie, even to his own ears.

Chief Miller simply stared, his mouth opening and closing like a fish. He gestured at the chaos around them – the scattered citizens, the tangled nets, the lingering scent of ozone. "Smoke, Gideon? You caused all *this* for smoke?" His voice was low, dangerous. "This is not reporting, Croft. This is... obstruction. This is criminal!"

Blackwood stepped forward, his presence even more menacing than Miller's fury. "He knew," Blackwood stated, his voice a low, chilling growl, his eyes never leaving Gideon's. "He knew the creature was there. He interfered. He is protecting it."

The words hung in the air, undeniable, damning. The citizens, now recovering from the initial panic, began to turn their bewildered, then suspicious, gazes towards Gideon. They had seen him sprint to the alarm. They had heard his flimsy excuse. They had seen the chaos erupt. And they had heard Blackwood's accusation.

Gideon felt their eyes, a hundred pinpricks of suspicion. The silence was deafening, save for the lingering echoes of the siren in his ears. He was no longer just the town's reporter, or even its eccentric oddity. He was now, irrevocably, publicly, the focus of their suspicion. He had saved Ingis. But in doing so, he had exposed himself completely. The loneliness of his secret had never felt so profound, nor so utterly dangerous. The hunt for

CHAPTER 28

the creature had just found a new, unexpected quarry: Gideon Croft.

Chapter 29

The silence that followed the fire alarm's dying wail in Oakhaven's town square was more damning than any accusation. It was the kind of silence that amplifies every unspoken thought, every flickering suspicion. Gideon Croft stood amidst the still-recovering chaos, the cuts on his palm stinging less than the searing gaze of Chief Miller and Silas Blackwood. He had saved Ingis, yes, but at the cost of his own carefully constructed anonymity. The jig, as they say, was well and truly up.

He didn't try to flee. There was nowhere to go. Miller's patrol car was blocking the nearest exit, and Blackwood's Unit, though still disoriented, was slowly regaining its composure, their eyes now firmly fixed on Gideon. The lingering scent of ozone, a phantom limb of Ingis's panic, hung in the crisp air, an invisible witness to his interference.

"Croft," Chief Miller's voice was dangerously low, a stark contrast to his earlier bellow. He was no longer purple with fury; he was cold, methodical, and profoundly disappointed. "My office. Now."

There was no negotiation, no argument. Gideon simply nodded, his shoulders slumped. He walked to Miller's patrol car, the Unit members parting for him like water, their stares a palpable weight. Blackwood remained rooted by the fountain, his gaze following Gideon, a silent, grim promise of future reckoning.

The drive to the police station was excruciating. Chief Miller drove in silence, his knuckles white on the steering wheel. The rhythmic *thump-thump* of the tires on the asphalt seemed to mock Gideon, each revolution bringing him closer to an inescapable confrontation. Gideon stared out the window at the familiar Oakhaven streets, now seen through the lens of his inevitable exposure. Every house, every shop, every park bench felt like a place he had betrayed.

At the station, Miller led him directly into his cramped, utilitarian office. The smell of stale coffee and paperwork was a stark reminder of Gideon's own discarded reality. Miller sat heavily behind his desk, not bothering to offer Gideon a seat. The donut box remained unopened. This was serious.

"Sit down, Gideon," Miller finally said, his voice flat.

Gideon pulled up the rickety chair, the same one he'd sat in countless times, interviewing Miller about petty crimes and local initiatives. Now, the roles were reversed.

Miller leaned back, his eyes fixed on Gideon. "Let's be clear, Gideon. That wasn't an 'emergency.' That wasn't 'smoke.' That was deliberate. You caused a public panic. You obstructed a police operation. You interfered with the Neighborhood Watch and Creature Containment Unit." He paused, letting each accusation hang in the air. "And you did it to allow something to escape."

Gideon's throat was dry. "Chief, I..."

"Don't lie to me, Gideon," Miller interrupted, his voice hardening. "Not anymore. I've gone along with your 'master illusionist' theories. I've entertained your 'static squirrels.' I've given you the benefit of every doubt. But what happened out there? That was too much. You acted like you were protecting something. Something *real*."

Miller stood up and walked to the filing cabinet, pulling out the slim folder Gideon recognized as his own anomaly log. He slammed it gently onto the desk. "Mrs. Gable's thimbles. Mr. Henderson's watch. The clock tower key. The prize ribbon. All of it. And every single time, Gideon, you were either the first on the scene, or you just happened to be in the vicinity. Every single time, you offered a convenient, yet ultimately flimsy, explanation. Every single time, you tried to steer me away from the truth."

He opened the folder and pointed to an entry. "The botanical garden. You destroyed property. You claimed it was a crow. A crow that happens to trigger sophisticated net traps?" Miller's voice rose slightly, edged with disbelief. "And then today. You caused a full-blown public panic. For what, Gideon? To let what escape?"

Gideon remained silent, his gaze fixed on the scuff marks on the linoleum floor. He couldn't deny it. The evidence, seen through Miller's pragmatic lens, was overwhelming.

"I trusted you, Gideon," Miller continued, his voice softening, but with a deeper sting of betrayal. "I saw you as a good, honest reporter. Maybe a little cynical, but honest. I looked to you for insight. You were my eyes and ears on the ground. And all this time, you've been... actively deceiving me. Actively hiding something."

Miller walked around the desk, leaning against the edge, closer to Gideon. "Let me tell you something, Gideon. The people in this town are scared. They're looking for answers. And now, thanks to your little stunt today, they're looking at *you*. Silas Blackwood, he's not a fool. He's already told me he believes you are actively protecting this… this *creature*."

Gideon finally looked up, meeting Miller's gaze. "Chief, it's not what you think…"

"Isn't it?" Miller countered, his voice sharp. "Because what I think, Gideon, is that you know exactly what's behind all these incidents. What I think is that you have personal knowledge of it. And what I think is that you just aided and abetted something that could be a significant danger to this community."

He paused, letting his words sink in. "Your objectivity, Gideon, is completely compromised. You're not reporting the news; you're *making* it. You're part of the story now. And that's a very dangerous place for a journalist to be."

Miller straightened up, walking back to his desk. His tone shifted, becoming more formal, more official. "Now, I can bring you in for obstruction of a police investigation. I can bring you in for reckless endangerment, given the panic you caused. I can certainly investigate you for aiding and abetting the perpetrator of these thefts and disturbances."

Gideon felt a cold knot of fear. Legal consequences. This was no longer just about public perception; this was about his freedom, his career, his entire future.

"But I'm not going to do that," Miller said, his voice measured. "Not yet. Because a part of me, Gideon, still believes there's a reason for all this. A reason you're so desperate to keep it secret. But my patience is worn thin. My trust in you is hanging by a thread."

He picked up a pen, tapping it against the desk. "Here's how this is going to work. You're going to tell me what you know. Everything. From the beginning. And you're going to tell me now. Or, Gideon, I will have no choice but to proceed with formal charges. And believe me, with Blackwood breathing down my neck, and the entire town convinced something unnatural is afoot, I will throw the book at you. You caused widespread panic. That won't go unpunished."

Gideon looked at the resolute face of Chief Miller. The kindly, slightly oblivious Chief had vanished, replaced by a stern, unyielding lawman. The guilt of his deception, of misleading this honest man, crashed over him anew. He had always known this moment might come, but the reality was far more crushing than he had anticipated. He had protected Ingis. But now, his own freedom, and perhaps Ingis's ultimate safety, depended on a choice: confess, and risk Ingis's capture, or continue the impossible lie, and face the full force of Oakhaven's justice system. The weight of his secret had never felt so heavy, nor the stakes so terrifyingly high.

Chapter 30

The air in Chief Miller's cramped office was thick with unspoken words, with suspicion, and with the desperate weight of Gideon Croft's secret. The Chief's ultimatum hung in the stale air like a death sentence: confess, or face criminal charges. Gideon looked at the resolute, weary face of the man across from him, a man who had trusted him, a man he had deeply betrayed. The kind, bumbling Chief had vanished, replaced by a lawman whose patience had finally snapped.

He could lie. He could continue to spin elaborate tales, to deny, to obfuscate. But the conviction in Miller's eyes, the cold, hard logic of Blackwood's accusation, told him it was futile. The net had tightened too much. His elaborate dance of misdirection had run its course. And more importantly, the image of Ingis, terrified and exposed during the fire alarm incident, flashed in his mind. He couldn't protect it if he was behind bars. He couldn't protect it if Oakhaven remained blind to the truth, chasing shadows while the real threat of containment loomed.

A different kind of desperation settled over him. What if... what if telling the truth, the impossible truth, was the *only* way to save Ingis? He had spent months trying to protect its existence from the world. Now, perhaps, he had to trust one small piece of that world. He had to gamble everything on Chief

Miller's inherent decency, his pragmatism, and his surprising openness to Gideon's bizarre "theories."

Gideon took a deep, shuddering breath. "Chief," he began, his voice hoarse, "what I know... it's going to sound completely unbelievable. You're going to think I've lost my mind."

Miller merely watched him, his expression unreadable. "Try me, Gideon. After the past few months in Oakhaven, 'unbelievable' is starting to sound like a Tuesday."

Gideon hesitated, a battle raging within him. This was the point of no return. The end of his journalistic facade. The revelation of the impossible. He thought of Ingis's iridescent scales, its playful chirps, its innocent pursuit of shine. He thought of the deep, unspoken bond they had forged. He couldn't betray that. He had to choose his words carefully, to present the truth in a way that wouldn't immediately lead to panic and pursuit.

"It's not an illusionist, Chief," Gideon finally said, his voice gaining a strange, fragile strength. "And it's not a static squirrel. It's... it's a creature."

Miller's eyes narrowed, but he didn't interrupt. He simply waited, his gaze unwavering.

"It's tiny, Chief. No bigger than my hand. Emerald green scales, iridescent. It has small, leathery wings. And it... it breathes fire. Not in a destructive way, not intentionally. It's more like... like a sneeze. When it's startled, or excited." Gideon spoke rapidly now, as if trying to outrun his own disbelief. "And it has an insatiable desire for shiny objects. Especially those with sentimental value. That's why the thimbles, the watch, the key... they all have meaning to people. It's drawn to that."

Miller listened, his expression slowly shifting from skepticism to a profound, almost comical, bewilderment. His mouth, usually set in a firm line, hung slightly agape.

"A... a tiny, fire-breathing... creature?" Miller finally managed to articulate, his voice a disbelieving whisper. "Gideon, are you telling me you've seen a... a dragon?"

Gideon nodded, a strange sense of relief washing over him, despite the absurdity of the confession. "Yes, Chief. A dragon. Its name is Ingis."

Miller pushed away from his desk, standing up slowly. He walked to the window, staring out at the quiet Oakhaven street as if searching for something, anything, to ground him back in reality. "A dragon," he repeated, his voice flat, devoid of emotion. "In Oakhaven. All this time, I thought it was kids. Or a very determined magpie. Fitzwilliam... Fitzwilliam was right?"

"In a very garbled way, yes," Gideon admitted. "He saw glimpses. He interpreted them through his... unique lens. Dr. Thorne's report, with its 'unidentified biological agent' – that's Ingis, too."

Miller turned, his eyes wide. "Thorne... he's talking about a dragon?"

"He doesn't know it's a dragon," Gideon clarified quickly. "He just knows it's an unknown biological entity leaving these unique scorch marks and taking shiny objects. He's investigating scientifically. He'll want to study it. Capture it. That's why I had to... interfere."

Miller slumped back into his chair, running a hand over his face. He looked utterly flummoxed, like a man who had just been told the sky was purple. "My God, Gideon. This is... this is impossible."

"I know," Gideon said, his voice softening. "Believe me, I thought so too. But I've seen it, Chief. I've spent months observing it. It's not malicious. It's just... following its instincts.

It's a magnificent, innocent creature. And it's vulnerable. If Blackwood's Unit finds it, if the town panics, it could be killed. Or worse, captured and experimented on."

Miller remained silent for a long moment, his gaze fixed on nothing in particular. Gideon watched him, his heart in his throat. This was the gamble. This was the moment Miller either believed him or had him committed.

Finally, Miller looked at Gideon, a flicker of something new in his eyes – not anger, not skepticism, but a dawning realization, a bewildered acceptance of the truly extraordinary. "So, that's why you've been acting like a madman. The botanical garden. The fire alarm. All of it... to protect this... Ingis?"

Gideon nodded. "Yes, Chief. It was the only way. I couldn't let them get it. It's harmless, truly. It just... collects."

Miller slowly pushed himself up from his desk. "Gideon," he said, his voice still low, "I'm going to ask you to do something. Something that goes against everything I've ever believed. I want to see it."

Gideon felt a surge of adrenaline, a mix of fear and desperate hope. This was it. The ultimate test of trust. "Now, Chief? Here?"

"No," Miller said, shaking his head. "Not here. Too risky. And not with Blackwood breathing down my neck. We need to do this... discreetly. Somewhere controlled. Your apartment."

Gideon nodded, relief flooding him. Miller was willing to see. He was willing to believe. "Okay, Chief. Tonight. Just you. No one else."

"Agreed," Miller said, his voice firm. "But Gideon, if this is some kind of elaborate hoax... if you're playing me for a fool..." His gaze hardened slightly, a warning.

"It's not, Chief," Gideon assured him. "You'll see."

CHAPTER 30

They agreed on a time, late that night, after Oakhaven had gone to sleep. Gideon left the station, the cuts on his palm throbbing. He felt an immense sense of relief, but also a terrifying vulnerability. He had placed Ingis's secret, its very existence, in the hands of Chief Miller. The trust was immense, the risk even greater.

He returned to his apartment, the mundane surroundings now feeling charged with an almost sacred purpose. He meticulously cleaned, set out fresh water, and carefully arranged a few of Ingis's favorite (and less incriminating) shiny objects near the balcony door. He needed Ingis to be comfortable, to trust Miller. He tried to mentally prepare Ingis, speaking softly to the empty room, explaining that a friend would visit, someone who needed to understand.

As the appointed hour approached, Gideon paced his apartment, his nerves stretched taut. He looked out his window at the darkened town. Somewhere out there, Blackwood's Unit was patrolling, unaware of the revelation that was about to unfold. Somewhere else, Dr. Thorne was perhaps analyzing new samples, unknowingly inching closer to the very truth Gideon was about to reveal.

A soft knock came at his door, precisely on time. Gideon took a deep breath and opened it. Chief Miller stood there, alone, his face etched with a mixture of curiosity and deep-seated apprehension. He was off-duty, in civilian clothes, a rare sight that emphasized the personal, unprecedented nature of this meeting.

"Chief," Gideon said, stepping aside.

Miller walked into the apartment, his eyes immediately scanning the room, perhaps expecting some elaborate trick. He stopped by the coffee table, his gaze falling on the small, iridescent scale Gideon had kept there. He reached out a trembling hand and carefully picked it up.

"This is...?" Miller began, his voice a low whisper.

"From Ingis," Gideon confirmed. "It sheds them sometimes."

Just then, a faint, bell-like chirrup came from the direction of Gideon's bookshelf. Miller's head snapped up.

Ingis, sensing a quiet presence, slowly emerged from behind a stack of books, its emerald scales shimmering in the lamplight. It peered out, its fiery eyes blinking, assessing the new human in its space. It chirped again, a soft, questioning sound, then took a single, cautious step towards them.

Chief Miller froze, the iridescent scale still clutched in his hand. His eyes, wide with utter astonishment, fixed on the tiny dragon. He stared, completely motionless, his breath seemingly caught in his throat. The pragmatic Chief Miller, the man of logic and reason, was utterly, irrevocably stunned. The impossible reality of Ingis, alive and vibrant in Gideon's living room, had rendered him speechless. His mind, Gideon knew, was reeling, trying to reconcile everything he had ever known with the extraordinary truth now fluttering before his very eyes. The secret was out. And the future of Ingis, and Oakhaven, now hung in the balance of Miller's next breath.

Chapter 31

Chief Miller stood frozen, the tiny, iridescent scale clutched in his hand, his eyes wide and unblinking, fixed on the emerald-green creature that had emerged from behind Gideon's bookshelf. The air in the apartment crackled with the impossible, the mundane reality of Gideon's living room momentarily suspended. The pragmatic Chief of Police, a man whose life revolved around indisputable facts and the measurable world, was confronted with a living myth. His breath, seemingly caught in his throat, finally escaped in a slow, disbelieving exhale.

Ingis, sensing the Chief's stillness, chirped again, a soft, questioning sound, then took another cautious step forward, its fiery eyes blinking at Miller with an innocent curiosity. It tilted its head, observing the human with the same intense scrutiny Miller usually reserved for crime scenes.

"My God," Miller whispered, the words barely audible. He wasn't speaking to Gideon; he was speaking to himself, to the shattered fragments of his worldview. "It's... it's real." His gaze darted from Ingis to the scale in his hand, then back to the dragon, as if trying to reconcile the tangible evidence with the impossible reality. His mind, usually a well-ordered file cabinet of facts, was reeling, attempting to categorize something that defied all known categories.

Gideon watched him, his heart pounding a nervous rhythm. This was the moment. Would Miller revert to his pragmatic training? Would he call for backup, for containment, for a report to the state authorities? Or would he see what Gideon saw: not a threat, but a wonder?

Slowly, Chief Miller knelt, his movements deliberate, almost reverent. Ingis, curious, took another step towards him, its tiny snout sniffing the air. Miller extended his free hand, palm open, offering no threat. Ingis hesitated for a moment, then, with a delicate flutter of its wings, landed softly on Miller's outstretched palm.

Miller's breath hitched again. He stared at the minuscule dragon, its emerald scales shimmering under the lamplight, its tiny, delicate claws gripping his skin, its infinitesimal puffs of smoke tickling his palm. The sight of it, so impossibly real, so utterly otherworldly, rendered the Chief speechless. He turned his gaze to Gideon, his eyes filled with a mixture of profound astonishment, bewildered awe, and a dawning understanding.

"All those reports," Miller finally said, his voice husky with emotion. "The scorch marks. The missing objects. Fitzwilliam's rants... Gideon, you weren't crazy. You were protecting... *this*."

Gideon nodded, a wave of relief washing over him so profound it almost made him lightheaded. Miller believed him. He truly, genuinely believed.

Chief Miller remained kneeling for a long moment, simply observing Ingis. His professional training, his years of rational problem-solving, were kicking in, but on an entirely new, unprecedented level. He saw the sheer scientific significance of the discovery. This wasn't just an animal; it was a living, breathing enigma, a creature that defied known biology, potentially rewriting the very laws of natural history. The ethical implications of its existence, and its potential discovery by the wider world, were immense. It wasn't just Oakhaven's peace at stake; it was Ingis's very survival.

"Its scales," Miller murmured, gently stroking Ingis with a trembling finger. "This is... this is groundbreaking, Gideon. And terrifying. If the wrong people find out..." He didn't need to finish the sentence. Gideon knew. Laboratories, dissection tables, cages.

Miller carefully stood, Ingis still perched on his hand. He walked to Gideon's map of Oakhaven, the one crisscrossed with anomaly locations. His gaze lingered on the mark of the clock tower key. "And the hoard," he said, turning to Gideon. "You found it, didn't you?"

Gideon nodded, and in a low voice, described the secret passage in the library, the glittering trove within. Miller listened intently, his scientific curiosity clearly piqued despite the inherent danger.

"Right," Miller said, his voice firming, the pragmatic Chief of Police beginning to reassert himself, but now with a completely new set of priorities. "This changes everything. My initial plan was to arrest you, Gideon. To bring you in. But now... now I understand. You were protecting it." He looked at Ingis, still nestled calmly in his palm, then at Gideon. "And you were right. We have to protect it. From Blackwood. From Thorne. From... everyone."

An unlikely alliance was forged in Gideon's small apartment that night, an unspoken pact between a cynical journalist and a bewildered but resolute police chief. They sat for hours, whispering in the hushed silence of the late night, devising a plan to protect Ingis from the very town they were sworn to serve.

"First," Miller stated, setting Ingis gently back on the bookshelf, the dragon immediately resuming its casual polishing of a silver earring, "we need to manage the narrative. Your articles, Gideon, they're going to be critical. You need to subtly shift public perception, to undermine Blackwood's 'creature' narrative, and, ironically, to subtly reinforce the idea that whatever is happening, it's not truly dangerous."

Gideon nodded, already thinking of angles. "I can focus on the 'prankster' angle again, Chief. Emphasize the lack of actual harm, the low value of most of the items. Frame it as a town mystery, a harmless game of cat and mouse."

"Good," Miller said. "And the scorch marks? We need to keep providing alternative explanations. Faulty wiring. Electrical surges. Anything plausible, however stretched."

Their next priority was Blackwood's Unit. "Blackwood is methodical," Miller explained, pacing the small living room. "He'll analyze. He'll learn. We need to disrupt his data. His thermal cameras, his sonic sensors... they need to be feeding him false information. Or no information."

Gideon outlined his previous, frantic attempts at sabotage – the foil over lenses, the disabled sonic disruptors. "It's a constant battle, Chief. He upgrades, I adapt. But I can't be everywhere."

"You won't have to be," Miller said, a grim determination setting in. "I can leverage my position. I can 'reallocate' Unit resources. Send them on wild goose chases. Prioritize areas that are deliberately clear of... any 'biological agents.'" He tapped a finger on Gideon's Oakhaven map. "We need to identify key safe zones for Ingis. Areas where it can collect without being detected. And we need to lure it there."

The golden clock tower key was a critical point. "The key needs to go back, Gideon," Miller stated. "Its absence is too high-profile. It fuels the fear. It proves Blackwood's point."

"I know," Gideon said. "But Ingis won't just give it up. Its hoard is its sanctuary. And it's driven by that desire for meaningful shine."

"Then we need to offer it something *more* appealing," Miller mused, his mind already working through possibilities. "Something just as shiny, but completely harmless. And we need a place to put it. A controlled environment where Ingis can indulge its instincts without endangering itself or the town." He looked around Gideon's apartment. "Your place is too small, too vulnerable."

They discussed potential new sanctuaries: the disused library passage, once a hiding place, now a potential controlled environment. Miller, with his knowledge of town infrastructure, suggested the old municipal vault, long empty and forgotten beneath the town hall. "It's secure, isolated," he reasoned. "And it's full of old, dusty filing cabinets. Perfect for a tiny creature to hide in, if we can make it enticing."

The ethical implications weighed heavily on Miller. "Gideon, we're essentially lying to an entire town. This is... highly irregular. I'm jeopardizing my career. My reputation." He looked at the tiny dragon, still contentedly polishing its earring. "But looking at it... knowing what Blackwood and Thorne would do... I don't see another choice."

"We're doing it to protect something truly extraordinary, Chief," Gideon said, a profound conviction in his voice. "Something the world isn't ready for."

They talked late into the night, their whispers filling the quiet apartment. They devised contingency plans, coded signals, and subtle ways to communicate without raising suspicion. Miller outlined strategies for using his authority to pull Blackwood's Unit in different directions, to subtly discredit Fitzwilliam by emphasizing the "psychological impact of fear." Gideon sketched out articles that would gradually shift public perception, portraying the "anomalies" as a harmless, albeit frustrating, local eccentricity rather than a terrifying threat.

As dawn approached, a faint light beginning to seep through the blinds, Miller finally stood. He looked utterly exhausted, but a new spark, a quiet determination, shone in his eyes. He had accepted the impossible. He had chosen to protect.

"Alright, Gideon," Miller said, his voice firm, "this alliance of ours... it has to remain a complete secret. From everyone. Brenda, your mother, even Thorne, if we can help it. Especially Blackwood. If anyone finds out, not only are we both finished, but Ingis... Ingis doesn't stand a chance."

Gideon nodded, a silent promise. The weight of his secret had not lessened, but it was now shared, a burden lightened by the unexpected bond with Chief Miller. The hunt for Ingis was still on, but now, the tiny dragon had a powerful, if unlikely, new ally. The future of Oakhaven, and its remarkable, secret resident, hung precariously in the balance, resting on the shoulders of a cynical journalist and a bewildered police chief. Their impossible task had just begun.

As they rounded the corner onto Main Street, a large, unexpected crowd was already gathering, drawn like moths to a flame. The flickering, harsh glow of portable floodlights illuminated the steps of the municipal hall, where a makeshift podium had been hastily erected. The air hummed not with the usual comfortable chatter of Oakhaven, but with a desperate, almost feverish anticipation, an unsettling buzz that prickled Gideon's skin, setting his teeth on edge.

"What in God's name is going on?" Miller mumbled, his brow furrowed with confusion and dawning apprehension. He scanned the throng of people, then the podium. "Another town meeting? Thompson didn't mention anything to me. This is highly irregular."

"Looks like Blackwood's doing," Gideon said, a cold premonition seizing him, a knot tightening in his stomach. He saw Blackwood standing tall and unmoving on the podium, his figure imposing even from a distance, radiating a grim, unyielding authority that somehow silenced the murmurs of the crowd, drawing all attention to himself. He was a general addressing his troops before battle.

They pushed their way through the fringes of the gathering, the sheer volume of people astonishing Gideon. The town hall, already accustomed to emergency meetings, was packed, overflowing onto the steps and sidewalk, a sea of anxious faces. But this time, the atmosphere was palpably different. There was a desperate, almost feverish anticipation, a hunger for answers that transcended mere curiosity. Blackwood, radiating a grim, unyielding authority, took the stage. He didn't shout, didn't resort to theatrics; he spoke with a quiet, unwavering conviction that resonated deeply with the anxious crowd, lending his words an undeniable, chilling power.

"My fellow Oakhavenites," Blackwood began, his voice calm, cutting through the murmurs like a honed blade, "for too long, we have lived with unease. With fear. We have seen our cherished possessions vanish. We have seen our town scarred by inexplicable marks. We have been told to be calm, to trust in explanations that strain belief, explanations that defy common sense and insult our intelligence." He looked pointedly at Chief Miller, who now stood stiffly beside Gideon, his face etched with growing dismay, his lips pressed into a thin, grim line. Blackwood's gaze was a deliberate challenge.

"I stand before you tonight with irrefutable proof," Blackwood declared, his voice rising, gaining a terrible, almost hypnotic power. He held up a large, blown-up thermal image, starkly printed on a poster board. It was grainy, indistinct to the casual eye, but undeniable to anyone with Blackwood's unwavering conviction: a distinct, warm glow emanating from deep within the library's old stone walls, a precise heat signature unlike anything human or mechanical. "This is from the old library. This is the heat signature of the creature that has plagued our town. It is a living, breathing heat source, undeniable proof."

A collective gasp went through the crowd, a wave of stunned understanding, followed by murmurs of terrified recognition. Blackwood continued, his voice now a powerful crescendo. "Dr. Thorne's report, which many of you have read, spoke of an 'unidentified biological agent.' I can now tell you, unequivocally, that this agent has made its lair in the very heart of our history. In the Oakhaven Library. And it is there, right now, hiding in plain sight, mocking our efforts, waiting in the dark."

He played on their deepest fears, subtly referencing Fitzwilliam's earlier, seemingly crazy predictions, legitimizing them with his newfound, tangible evidence. "Old Man Fitzwilliam, whom many dismissed as a harmless lunatic, spoke of fire-breathing pixies. He was closer to the truth than any of us knew. This creature, whatever its true nature, breathes fire. It has shown its capabilities. It has caused panic. And it is a direct, undeniable threat to our peace and safety, to our children's security, to the very fabric of Oakhaven." His words struck deep, resonating with the anxieties that had been building for months.

He then transitioned seamlessly to a call to arms, painting a vivid picture of a decisive, final action. "We cannot live like this. We cannot allow this unknown entity to hold our town hostage, to steal our treasured past, to threaten our future. I propose we, the citizens of Oakhaven, launch a focused, decisive operation. Not a hunt to harm indiscriminately, but a controlled, thorough **containment**. We will sweep the library. We will bring this creature out. And we will restore peace and order to Oakhaven, once and for all."

A powerful wave of assent swept through the hall. The frightened, the frustrated, the bewildered – all found a common purpose in Blackwood's decisive, fear-driven leadership. They craved action, resolution, and Blackwood offered it with chilling conviction, a promise of an end to their collective nightmare.

Chief Miller, witnessing the horrifying scene unfold, pushed himself to his feet. His face was pale, his hands clenched into tight fists at his sides. "Silas! Hold on now! This is reckless! We don't know what we're dealing with! We need a measured approach! This isn't the way!" Miller's voice, usually authoritative, was strained, edged with a desperate, pleading urgency. He knew Blackwood's plan, fueled by raw fear and now seemingly irrefutable evidence, would put Ingis in grave, immediate danger. He appealed to the crowd, his gaze sweeping over the anxious faces, trying to break through the fervor. "This is highly irregular! We have official protocols for situations like this! This could lead to serious unforeseen consequences for everyone involved! Think, Oakhaven! Think before you act! Do not let fear rule your judgment!"

Blackwood turned to Miller, a look of utter contempt on his face. "Chief Miller, your office has proven incapable of handling this threat. For months, you've offered excuses, and allowed this... *thing* to run rampant in our town. The town has spoken. We cannot afford to wait for bureaucracy. We need action. Now. The people demand it." He then turned back to the crowd, raising his voice, his words amplified by the makeshift sound system, completely drowning out Miller's desperate protests. "All those who stand with me! All those who wish to see Oakhaven restored to peace and safety! Join me tomorrow, at dawn, at the library! We will face this threat together! This is our town, and we will reclaim it!"

The response was overwhelming. A roar of approval, a furious, collective shout of affirmation, a veritable forest of raised hands. The hall erupted in shouts of "Tomorrow!" and "For Oakhaven!" Miller's pleas for caution, his desperate attempts to calm the agitated crowd, his appeals to reason and protocol, were utterly drowned out by the thunderous wave of public support for Blackwood's decisive, fear-driven plan. He watched, horrified, as Blackwood effectively recruited a civilian army, bypassing his authority, leveraging the town's raw emotions and desperate desire for an end to their fear. His face was a picture of utter dismay, defeat, and a chilling recognition of the inevitable.

Gideon, standing at the back, felt a cold despair wash over him, a physical weight settling in his chest. His stomach churned. He had seen the precise thermal data Blackwood displayed. He knew Ingis was in there, curled up in its secret passage, oblivious to the terrifying verdict that had just been passed. He saw the zealous, almost feverish light in the volunteers' eyes, their grim, uncompromising determination.

CHAPTER 31

He looked at Chief Miller, defeated, isolated, his face a picture of despair. All their counter-measures, all their subtle diversions, all their whispered plans, had led to this. Blackwood had found Ingis's hiding spot. And now, the hunt for the mysterious creature was about to become a full-scale, public siege on the old town library. This was it. The final, unavoidable confrontation. He knew he had to get to the library, and warn Ingis, before the crowd dispersed and the dawn arrived. He had to run, to try and save Ingis, even if it meant leaving Miller to face the indignant crowd alone, trying to disperse the growing mob. The clock was ticking, and Ingis's time was running out.

Chapter 32

The first sliver of dawn, cold and unforgiving, pierced the pre-morning gloom, painting the skeletal branches of the Oakhaven Library's surrounding trees in stark, skeletal silhouettes. A thin layer of frost coated the ground, crunching softly underfoot as the Neighborhood Watch and Creature Containment Unit, bolstered by dozens of new, impassioned volunteers, assembled. The air, heavy with the scent of damp earth and the unspoken fears of the gathered townsfolk, vibrated with a raw, almost electric tension. Gideon Croft stood beside Chief Miller, his heart a frantic drumbeat against his ribs, each beat a silent prayer for the impossible creature hidden within the ancient walls.

Silas Blackwood, a figure of grim determination carved from granite, surveyed his expanded Unit. Dozens of volunteers, their faces etched with a grim resolve born of fear and civic duty, stood at attention. They were armed not with firearms, but with the tools of containment: collapsible nets with weighted edges, tranquilizer guns loaded with humane darts, and sophisticated tracking devices that pulsed with faint, almost imperceptible lights. Their silent formation, the precise spacing between them, was a chilling testament to Blackwood's meticulous planning, designed to leave no avenue of escape for the "creature"

CHAPTER 32

he was so determined to apprehend. He moved among them, a silent commander, his eyes scanning for any sign of hesitation, his presence a cold, unyielding force. The larger crowd of curious, anxious townsfolk, including the local media (Brenda, looking terrified but still clutching her notepad), hovered at a respectful distance, drawn by the unusual activity.

"Chief Miller," Blackwood's voice, calm and cutting, sliced through the tense silence, resonating with an authority that brooked no argument. "My Unit is ready. Your officers, I trust, will ensure the safety of the perimeter outside. We are proceeding with containment."

Miller, his face tired but resolute, met Blackwood's gaze. "My men are in position, Blackwood. But I reiterate, this is a containment, not a hunt. No unnecessary force." His voice was firm, a final, futile attempt to exert control.

Blackwood merely grunted, his eyes fixed on the imposing, heavy oak doors of the library. "Understood." His tone implied that "understood" merely meant acknowledged, not necessarily agreed with. "Unit Alpha, breach and clear. Unit Beta, establish inner perimeter."

The heavy oak doors of the library groaned open with a deep, resonant sound that echoed through the quiet morning. Blackwood led the way, his stride purposeful, his flashlight cutting a sharp beam through the dim interior. Four members of Unit Alpha followed, their faces masked by the shadows, their movements swift and silent. Gideon felt a wave of nausea. This was it. The moment of truth, the point of no return.

"Wait!" Gideon shouted, his voice hoarse, desperate, stepping forward before his mind could fully process the words. "Mr. Blackwood, there's something you need to understand! This isn't what you think!"

Blackwood paused, turning slowly, his eyes narrowed to unyielding slits. His patience, already stretched thin by Gideon's previous interference, was visibly wearing. "Step aside, Mr. Croft. This is a police matter, and a matter of public safety. Your interference ends here. You've caused enough chaos."

"He's right, Silas," Chief Miller added, stepping up beside Gideon, his hand resting briefly on Gideon's shoulder, a silent gesture of support. "There's... there's a misunderstanding here. We believe this can be resolved peacefully, without further alarm. Without... without force." Miller's voice held a careful ambiguity, trying to hint at the truth without explicitly revealing Ingis to Blackwood. He held Blackwood's gaze, trying to convey the gravity of his words through sheer force of will. "We've been through this, Silas. Aggression here could lead to unforeseen dangers. For your Unit. For the town. Let's reassess. There are other ways."

"Peacefully?" Blackwood scoffed, a sneer twisting his lips, utterly dismissing Miller's desperate plea. His gaze flicked to Gideon, then back to Miller, a spark of contempt in his eyes. "After months of thefts? After the clock tower key? After the chaos Mr. Croft caused in the square? There's nothing peaceful about this, Chief. There's a creature in there, and we're bringing it out. By whatever means necessary. My Unit's safety comes first, and that means securing this threat." His words were cold, uncompromising, a stone wall against Miller's reasoned argument. He waved his hand, a sharp, dismissive gesture. "Proceed!"

Unit Alpha moved deeper into the library, their footsteps echoing ominously in the vast, silent space, their flashlights dancing across dusty bookshelves and forgotten reading nooks. Gideon and Miller exchanged another quick, desperate glance.

CHAPTER 32

Their combined efforts had failed to deter Blackwood. They couldn't let Blackwood's force encounter Ingis unprepared, or worse, trigger its panic without a mediating presence. The outcome would be catastrophic for the tiny dragon, and potentially for Blackwood's team. Gideon felt the cold tendrils of helplessness creep up his spine.

They moved through the main reading room, past towering shelves of dusty tomes, the vastness of the space feeling strangely claustrophobic. The silence was punctuated only by the scuff of boots, the crackle of walkie-talkies, and the hushed commands of Blackwood, directing his men with unnerving precision. Gideon's heart was a lead weight in his chest. Where was Ingis? Had it somehow sensed the danger and flown?

Suddenly, a Unit member shouted, his voice echoing sharply through the cavernous library. "Over here! Near the local history section! I've got a hit! Thermal confirmed!"

Gideon's blood ran cold, a wave of icy dread washing over him. The secret passage. Blackwood's thermal camera had been accurate. It had pinpointed the heat signature of Ingis, nestled deep within its hoard, emanating a faint but persistent warmth even through stone.

Blackwood immediately strode towards the alcove, his expression grimly triumphant. Unit members converged on the area, their nets ready, their tranquilizer guns raised, their faces a mixture of apprehension and grim resolve. Gideon pushed past Chief Miller, a desperate cry forming in his throat.

"No! Wait! Don't corner it! You'll scare it!"

He burst into the alcove, just as Blackwood's team reached the concealed bookshelf. One of the Unit members, following Blackwood's precise instructions, located the hidden catch – the old book Gideon had used as a trigger. He pushed it, and with a soft, grinding groan of ancient wood and stone, the section of the bookshelf swung inward, revealing the dark, narrow passage.

A collective gasp went through the Unit. The scent of ozone, stronger now, almost palpable, wafted from the opening, mingling with the musty smell of old paper and dust.

"Creature in sight!" a Unit member yelled, his voice strained with a mixture of fear and awe, his flashlight beam cutting into the darkness of the passage.

Inside the passage, illuminated by their flashlights, Ingis was indeed there. It was perched in the very center of its glittering hoard, surrounded by a dazzling pile of Oakhaven's treasures – the golden clock tower key gleaming at its pinnacle, radiating a brilliant, almost hypnotic luster. Ingis, startled by the sudden breach of its sanctuary, its privacy brutally invaded by the blinding flashlights and human voices, let out a terrified, high-pitched chirrup. Its tiny body trembled uncontrollably, its iridescent scales seeming to lose some of their luster in its rising fear. Its fiery eyes were wide with confusion and mounting panic.

"Nets ready!" Blackwood commanded, his voice sharp, unwavering, devoid of any doubt. "Target acquired! Move in! Contain it!"

Gideon launched himself forward, a desperate, last-ditch attempt to intervene, to shield, to explain. "Don't! You'll scare it! It's harmless! It's only defensive!"

Miller lunged, grabbing Blackwood's arm, his grip surprisingly strong. "Blackwood, hold! It's just a creature reacting to fear! Think of the consequences!"

But Blackwood, his eyes fixed on his quarry, shook off Miller's grip with a powerful shrug. "Consequences? Chief, the town demands containment! It's what we promised! This is a menace! It's what the people want!" He gestured towards Ingis with his tranquilizer gun, ready to subdue.

As the Unit members, their faces grim, moved into the narrow passage, their nets extended like hungry shadows, their presence a suffocating, overwhelming threat, Ingis reached its breaking point. Cornered, terrified, its ancient instincts overriding everything Gideon had taught it, the tiny dragon unleashed a dramatic, yet ultimately harmless, burst of its primal power.

A blinding flash of emerald light erupted from the passage, filling the entire library with an ethereal, otherworldly glow. It wasn't a destructive fire, not a consuming inferno designed to burn or char, but a magnificent, awe-inspiring display of pure, concentrated light and heat. Flames, vibrant and shimmering with the colors of a thousand gemstones, danced and flickered around Ingis, illuminating its scales with an impossible brilliance, its delicate wings unfurling in a burst of pure, raw energy. The heat rippled outwards in a tangible wave, a sudden, intense warmth that forced the Unit members closest to stumble back, their faces shielded, their nets dropping uselessly to the floor. The air crackled, not just with ozone, but with the raw power of a myth made real. A deafening whoosh filled the space, then dissipated into a stunned silence.

The display lasted only a few seconds, a magnificent, terrifying spectacle of light and sound, utterly overwhelming in its unexpected beauty and power. Then, as quickly as it had begun, the light faded, leaving the passage bathed once more in the dim, uncertain glow of flashlights.

Ingis was still there, perched amidst its now-glowing hoard, its tiny body heaving, visibly exhausted, its nostrils still emitting faint wisps of smoke. But it was no longer hidden. It was exposed, revealed in its full, impossible glory to Chief Miller, to Silas Blackwood, and to every stunned member of the Unit, who stood frozen, their mouths agape, their minds reeling from the impossible, fiery display they had just witnessed. The creature was real. And it was a dragon.

Chapter 33

The profound silence that descended upon the old Oakhaven Library after Ingis's dramatic, fiery display was absolute, shattered only by the ragged breathing of the Unit members and the faint, ringing echo that lingered in Gideon Croft's ears. The air still carried the acrid, sweet scent of ozone and burnt sugar, a potent, tangible testament to the impossible spectacle they had just witnessed. Blackwood's Unit, once a disciplined force, stood utterly frozen, their nets abandoned, their tranquilizer guns lowered, their faces pale with a mixture of profound shock, bewildered terror, and an undeniable, primal awe that rooted them to the spot.

Ingis, exhausted by its outburst, remained perched amidst its glittering hoard, its tiny body trembling visibly from the exertion, its fiery eyes wide and disoriented, reflecting the residual light of the flashlights. The golden clock tower key, still at the pinnacle of its treasure pile, reflected the remaining flashlight beams with an almost mocking brilliance, a silent witness to the earth-shattering reveal.

Then, the chaos erupted. Not a physical chaos, but a mental one. Whispers started, then grew louder, escalating quickly into a cacophony of shouts. "It's... it's a dragon!" someone shrieked, their voice high-pitched with terror and disbelief.

"My God, Fitzwilliam was right! It's a real dragon!" another cried, a hysterical edge to their tone. "It breathes fire!" "It's going to burn us all!" Fear, raw, instinctive, and unbridled, gripped the Unit members. Some took a hesitant step back, others fumbled frantically for their radios, their faces contorted with a disbelief that warred with the undeniable evidence before their eyes. The disciplined containment unit, built on logical principles, dissolved into a disorganized, terrified crowd, their formation broken.

"Silence!" Blackwood roared, his voice strained, raw with a desperate urgency to regain control, even as his own face was a mask of furious disbelief. He stared at Ingis, his hunter's instincts, honed over years of tracking tangible beasts, utterly overwhelmed by the sight of a living myth, by the creature that defied all his accumulated knowledge. He still clutched his tranquilizer gun, but his hand, he noticed, was trembling uncontrollably.

It was Chief Miller who stepped into the breach, his movements quiet, authoritative, cutting through the burgeoning panic. He pushed past the stunned Unit members, his gaze fixed on Ingis, a profound sense of protective responsibility overriding any personal fear. He didn't carry a weapon, only the weight of his office and his new, impossible knowledge.

"Everyone, calm yourselves!" Miller's voice, though not loud, carried a calm, authoritative tone that, against all odds, managed to cut through the rising hysteria. He stood at the threshold of the secret passage, looking at Ingis, then at the bewildered, terrified Unit members, his gaze steady and reassuring.

"What... what is it, Chief?" a Unit member stammered, his face as pale as anyone's, his eyes fixed on Miller, searching for an anchor of rationality in the impossible, for an official explanation to grasp onto.

Miller turned, his gaze sweeping over the Unit, his composure unwavering. "This," he began, his voice clear and measured, resonating with a new, quiet authority, "is a creature of immense... *uniqueness*. My initial reports, and Dr. Thorne's preliminary research, referred to it as an 'unidentified biological agent.' I can now confirm it is indeed biological. And it appears to be a previously undocumented species of... well, it's a small dragon."

A ripple of renewed gasps and murmurs went through the Unit, the word "dragon" sparking a new wave of awe and fear. "A dragon?" someone whispered, their voice filled with a disbelieving wonder.

"Yes," Miller confirmed, unflustered by the reactions. "A dragon. A very small one, certainly. And as you have just witnessed, a highly reactive one. But understand this: its display of flame was a purely defensive reaction. It was startled, cornered, frightened by your sudden breach of its sanctuary. It is not malicious. Its behavior, its attraction to metallic, historically significant objects, points to an an innate, instinctual drive. A form of advanced, perhaps even ritualized, collection, not an act of aggression or malevolence against humanity."

He gestured towards the shimmering hoard within the passage, illuminated by the lingering flashlights. "This is not a monster hoarding gold for power, Mr. Blackwood. This is a creature simply fulfilling a deep, ancient biological imperative to collect and protect its perceived treasures. It is essentially harmless to humans unless directly provoked or threatened beyond its capacity for fear."

Blackwood, recovering from his initial shock, his face now a mask of furious indignation, finally found his voice. "Harmless? It breathes fire! It's been stealing property! It caused a panic in the town square! This thing is a menace, Chief! It needs to be contained! Permanently!" He tried to step forward, his tranquilizer gun raising slightly, a desperate glint in his eye.

"Contained, yes, Mr. Blackwood, but not as a threat," Chief Miller interjected, his voice firm, fully backing Gideon's earlier stance. The awe was still in his eyes, but it had solidified into conviction, born from holding Ingis in his own hand just nights before. He had seen Ingis up close, held it, witnessed its innocence. He knew Gideon was telling the truth. "This is not a beast to be hunted down. This is a scientific discovery. And a vulnerable creature that has shown no intent to harm."

Miller stepped forward, placing himself squarely between Blackwood and the passage entrance, his body a solid barrier. His uniform, his badge, his undeniable authority as Chief of Police commanded attention, forcing Blackwood to pause. "Neighborhood Watch and Creature Containment Unit! I am ordering you to stand down! Put your weapons away! Secure the perimeter, but no one is to approach that passage! This is an official police order!"

Blackwood's face flushed crimson with anger, his jaw clenched so tightly a muscle twitches in his temple. "Chief! This is absurd! We had it! We nearly had it contained! This is what the town voted for!"

"You nearly provoked a defenseless creature into a panic that could have led to unforeseen consequences for your own men," Miller retorted, his gaze unwavering, his voice stern. "We have seen the creature with our own eyes. This is not a threat that requires lethal force or aggressive tactics. Your Unit's mandate was containment, not extermination. And under my authority as Chief of Police, I am re-evaluating the containment protocol. This creature is now under my protection."

The Unit members looked at each other, confused, their weapons still lowered. Their leader, Blackwood, was furious, his face a thundercloud. But their Chief of Police, a man they respected for his steady hand, was giving a direct order, backed by the undeniable visual proof. The chain of command, in this moment, was clear.

"Are you backing this, Chief?" one Unit member asked, his voice still wavering, but his gaze fixed on Miller, awaiting the final word.

"I am," Miller confirmed, his voice leaving no room for doubt. "This creature is not to be harmed. It is to be observed, understood, and protected. That is the new directive."

Blackwood, humiliated, his face a mask of furious disbelief and impotent rage, took a single, controlled step back. His eyes, cold and hard as flint, fixed on Gideon Croft. "You," he growled, the word a guttural sound of pure hatred, a silent promise of revenge in his tone. "You knew. You protected it. You will regret this, Croft."

Gideon met his gaze, unflinching, a profound sense of relief washing over him, even as a fresh wave of anxiety about Blackwood's future actions sparked within him. He had saved Ingis. The truth was out, no longer a secret burden. And Chief Miller, seeing the undeniable reality of the tiny, extraordinary dragon, had chosen the path of protection, aligning himself with Gideon. The chaos in the library slowly began to subside, replaced by a stunned, disbelieving silence, as Oakhaven's Unit absorbed the impossible truth: the "monster" they hunted was real, and it was a wonder.

Chapter 34

The immediate aftermath of Ingis's public revelation in the old Oakhaven Library was a cacophony of confusion, wonder, and fear. Chief Miller's decisive order to stand down, backed by his own authoritative explanation, had prevented immediate disaster, but it couldn't erase the shock that had rippled through Blackwood's Unit and, by extension, the entire town. News, in Oakhaven, traveled faster than wildfire, and the tale of the "fire-breathing pixie" turning out to be a real, live, miniature dragon spread like lightning.

The library was immediately cordoned off, marked as an active "investigation zone" by Miller, ostensibly to keep the public out, but truly to keep Ingis's location secure. Gideon remained inside, an impromptu guardian, while Chief Miller faced the onslaught of questions from the press (the regional papers had descended, drawn by the earlier fire alarm chaos) and the bewildered citizens. Dr. Thorne, having witnessed the reveal and Miller's decisive action, quietly approached Miller, offering his scientific expertise and support, seeing a chance to study Ingis responsibly.

The town was instantly, irrevocably divided.

On one side were the **terrified**. These were the citizens who had dismissed Fitzwilliam as a lunatic, only to discover his wildest prophecies were rooted in a fiery reality. They imagined miniature dragons setting their homes ablaze, stealing their most precious heirlooms. They demanded immediate action, capture, or even extermination. "It's a menace!" cried Mrs. Henderson, her voice trembling. "It took my great-grandpappy's watch! Who knows what it'll do next?" They feared the unknown, the breach of their comfortable, predictable world. Fitzwilliam, ironically, became their unwilling figurehead, his earlier rants now seen as chilling foresight.

On the other side were the **awe-struck**. For these residents, the revelation of Ingis was a miracle, a glimpse of magic in a world that had become increasingly mundane. They spoke of its beauty, its iridescent scales, its delicate wings. They were captivated by the sheer impossibility of it, seeing it as a symbol of wonder, something to be cherished and protected. Children, less burdened by adult fears, were often the most captivated, their imaginations soaring with the idea of a real dragon in Oakhaven.

And then there were the **bewildered**. The vast majority of Oakhavenites simply couldn't process it. Their minds struggled to reconcile the tangible evidence—the scorch marks, the missing items—with the fantastical reality of a dragon. They swung between disbelief and reluctant acceptance, unsure how to react, how to feel, how to live in a town that was now home to a creature from myth.

Silas Blackwood was perhaps the most profoundly impacted. Humiliation, cold and bitter, settled upon him. His meticulously planned containment operation had ended in public disarray, his authority challenged by Chief Miller, his methodical approach undermined by a creature that defied all logic. He had been ridiculed by Fitzwilliam, contradicted by Miller, and his efforts rendered futile by Gideon. His pride, his very identity as a capable hunter and leader, had been shattered.

Gideon saw Blackwood later that day, his face grim, his eyes burning with a quiet, dangerous fury. "You knew," Blackwood stated, his voice a low, gravelly growl, fixing his gaze on Gideon. "You protected it. You made a fool of me, Croft. And you unleashed something dangerous onto this town. This isn't over. Not by a long shot." The vow of revenge was unspoken, but palpable. Blackwood, stripped of his authority, would become a formidable, persistent threat, now driven by personal grievance.

Gideon Croft, meanwhile, found himself in an unfamiliar, uncomfortable spotlight. To some, he was an accidental local hero, the one who knew the truth, the one who had bravely revealed and protected the miraculous creature. They lauded his "investigative courage" (ignoring, of course, the part where he'd tried to hide it for months). To others, particularly those who feared Ingis, and those who felt betrayed by his journalistic obfuscation, he was a controversial figure, a reckless individual who had knowingly harbored a "menace." His phone rang off the hook, besieged by calls from regional and even national news outlets, all demanding interviews, details, exclusive access to the "Oakhaven Dragon."

Brenda, his editor, was in a state of simultaneous shock and frantic excitement. "Gideon! A dragon! You knew about a dragon! This is the biggest story in Oakhaven history! Possibly national history! Why didn't you tell me?!" Her initial anger quickly gave way to a journalistic frenzy. She wanted an exclusive, a tell-all, everything.

Gideon felt the immense pressure, the shifting sands beneath his feet. His career, once stagnant, was now rocketing into an

CHAPTER 34

unforeseen trajectory. But with newfound fame came scrutiny. He had saved Ingis, but the town was bleeding from the shock, divided, and potentially dangerous. The aftermath was only just beginning, and Gideon knew that the fight to protect Ingis, to reshape Oakhaven's understanding of its extraordinary resident, was far from over.

Chapter 35

The old Oakhaven Library, once a quiet repository of forgotten stories, now hummed with a different kind of magic. Sunlight, streaming through its tall, arched windows, illuminated the subtle shimmer from within Ingis's sanctuary, a quiet, constant reminder of the extraordinary life within. Years had passed since Ingis's public revelation, since the town had transformed from mundane to magical. Gideon Croft, no longer the gaunt, perpetually anxious figure he once was, moved through the sanctuary with a calm, practiced ease, his presence a comforting hum to the tiny dragon.

Ingis, now fully accustomed to its secure habitat, thrived. Its scales seemed to glow with a deeper emerald hue, its chirps were more varied, more expressive. It would often emerge from the hidden passage leading to its hoard, a tiny, glittering jewel against the backdrop of the specially designed rock formations and miniature trees that mimicked its natural environment.

Even after years of observation and scientific study by Dr. Thorne, Ingis's unique instinct for shiny, meaningful objects remained undimmed. The hoard, now meticulously cataloged by Thorne's team, continued to grow, a testament to Ingis's persistent desire for new acquisitions. The golden clock tower key remained its central, most cherished piece, often found

CHAPTER 35

nestled closest to Ingis when it slept.

Gideon would often bring Ingis new, shiny offerings. Not stolen items, of course, but carefully selected, harmless trinkets: polished sea glass, sparkling geodes, the occasional piece of fool's gold. Ingis would accept them with a gentle sniff, sometimes batting at them playfully, but its discerning taste for *meaningful* shine remained.

One quiet afternoon, Gideon sat on a bench outside the sanctuary's viewing area, observing Ingis through the one-way glass. The tiny dragon was meticulously polishing a newly acquired item – a gleaming silver thimble, identical to one of Mrs. Gable's originals. Gideon chuckled softly. He knew that thimble. He had carefully selected a polished, identical replica and subtly placed it near the old library's entrance just the week before, a small, harmless lure that had delighted Ingis. It was a private, ongoing game between them.

Ingis, content in its sanctuary, still occasionally tried to "borrow" objects from Gideon's person during his visits. A glinting pen, a shiny button on his shirt, even the polished buckle of his belt. Gideon would playfully bat its snout away, a familiar routine between them. "Oh no you don't, little thief," he'd murmur, his voice filled with amused exasperation. Ingis would chirp, then dart away, sometimes leaving a small, perfectly polished pebble in its place as a silent offering.

Gideon, no longer the cynical journalist, found profound joy and purpose in his new, extraordinary life. His articles, now respected globally, focused on conservation, ethical coexistence, and the boundless wonders of the natural world. He had found his true calling, not in exposing the mundane, but in championing the miraculous. The weariness that had once defined him had been replaced by a quiet contentment, a sense of belonging to something far greater than himself.

Oakhaven, once a town struggling with its identity, had fully embraced its unique destiny. Tourism continued to thrive, bringing prosperity and new faces, but the core of Oakhaven remained intact: a small, tight-knit community that had learned to live with the impossible. The children of Oakhaven grew up knowing a real dragon lived amongst them, their imaginations forever sparked by the emerald flash and the stories of Ingis.

Chief Miller, now nearing retirement, often visited the sanctuary, standing beside Gideon, a silent observer of the miracle he had once struggled to believe. He sometimes spoke of the impossible choice Gideon had forced him to make, always with a grateful shake of his head. Dr. Thorne, a renowned expert in cryptobiology, continued his research, forever fascinated by the creature that defied all his textbooks.

And Old Man Fitzwilliam? He still rambled, but now, his pronouncements about "fire-imps" and "glittering gnomes" were met not with ridicule, but with fond, knowing smiles. He was the town's eccentric prophet, a living legend who had, against all odds, been proven right.

As evening fell, casting a soft, golden glow through the library windows, Gideon looked at Ingis, nestled safely within its shimmering sanctuary. The world outside still full of challenges, of conflicts, of cynicism. But in Oakhaven, a glimmer of magic had found a home. And because of a tiny, mischievous dragon named Ingis, the world was, undeniably, a little more magical, a little more wondrous, than it had been before. And Gideon Croft, its unlikely guardian, wouldn't have it any other way.

Also By Tristyn Barberi

- **Neon Shadows**
City Of Whispers
City Of Sorrow
- **Standalone Books**
Curious Cinders

About the Author

Tristyn Barberi is a serving member of the United States Navy who has embarked on a new and exciting adventure: the world of writing. Finding joy and creative expression in crafting stories, Tristyn approaches authorship with the same dedication and discipline honed through naval service. While navigating the demands of military life, Tristyn carves out time to explore imaginative landscapes and bring compelling characters to life, writing purely for the love of it.

www.ingramcontent.com/pod-product-compliance
Lightning Source LLC
LaVergne TN
LVHW041811060526
838201LV00046B/1220